Nora Roberts is the *New York Times* bestselling author of more than one hundred and ninety novels. A born storyteller, she creates a blend of warmth, humour and poignancy that speaks directly to her readers and has earned her almost every award for excellence in her field. The youngest of five children, Nora Roberts lives in western Maryland. She has two sons.

Visit her website at www.noraroberts.com

Nora Roberts

Time Was

MILLS & BOON

Published in Great Britain 2016
By Mills & Boon, an imprint of HarperCollins*Publishers*
1 London Bridge Street, London, SE1 9GF

HarperCollins*Publishers*
Macken House, 39/40 Mayor Street Upper
Dublin 1, D01 C9W8, Ireland

Time Was © 1989 Nora Roberts

ISBN: 978-0-263-92366-7

For Joan and Tom
Just for fun

Chapter 1

He was going down. The instrument panel was a maze of wildly flashing numbers and lights, and the cockpit was spinning like a merry-go-round gone mad. He didn't need the scream of warning bells to tell him he was in trouble. He didn't need the insistent red blip on his computer screen to tell him the trouble was big. He'd known that the moment he'd seen the void.

Swearing, clamping down on his panic, he struggled with the controls, using one hand to shove the lever forward for full power. The vehicle bucked and shuddered, fighting the gravitational pull. The Gs hit him like a wall. All around him metal screamed against metal.

"Hold together, baby," he managed to say as his lips stretched back over his teeth. The floor near his feet ripped open in a jagged line three inches long. "Hold together, you son of a—"

He jammed hard due east, swearing again when it seemed that no matter how cleverly he maneuvered he and his ship would be sucked into the hole.

The cockpit lights went out, leaving only the whirl of kaleidoscopic colors from the instrument panel. His ship went into a spiral, tumbling end over end like a stone fired from a slingshot. Now the light was white, hot and brilliant. Instinctively he threw up an arm to shield his eyes. The sudden crushing pressure on his chest left him helpless to do more than gasp for breath.

Briefly, before he lost consciousness, he remembered that his mother had wanted him to be a lawyer. But he'd just had to fly.

When he came to he was no longer spiraling—he was in a screaming free-fall. A glance at his instruments showed him only that they were damaged, the numbers racing backward. A new force had him plastered back against his seat, but he could see the curve of the earth.

Knowing he could pass out again at any moment, he lunged forward to knock the throttle back and turn the ship over to the computer. It would, he knew, scan for an unpopulated area, and if God was in His heaven the crash control in the old bucket would still be functional.

Maybe, just maybe, he'd live to see another sunrise. And how bad could practicing law be?

He watched the world rush toward him, blue and green and beautiful. The hell with it, he thought. Flying a desk would never be like this.

Libby stood on the porch of the cabin and watched the night sky boil. The wicked slices of lightning and the blowing curtain of rain were the best show in town. Even though she was standing under the overhang, her hair and her face were wet. Behind her, the lights in the cabin glowed a warm, cozy yellow. The next boom of thunder made her grateful she'd set out candles and kerosene lamps.

But the light and warmth didn't lure her back. Tonight she preferred the chill and the crashing power that was barreling through the mountains.

If the storm kept up much longer, it would be weeks before the north pass through the mountains was negotiable. It didn't matter, she thought as another spear of lightning split the sky. She had weeks. In fact, she thought with a grin, hugging herself against the brisk wind, she had all the time in the world.

The best decision she'd ever made had been to pack up and dig in at her family's hideaway cabin. She'd always had an affection for mountains. The Klamaths of southwestern Oregon had everything she wanted. A spectacular view, high, rugged peaks, pure air and solitude. If it took six months to write her dissertation on the effects of modernizing influences on the Kolbari Islanders, then so be it. She'd spent five years studying cultural anthropology, three of them in extensive fieldwork. She hadn't let up on herself since her eighteenth birthday, and she certainly hadn't given herself any time alone, away from family, studies and other scientists. The dissertation was important to her—too important, she could sometimes admit. Coming here to work alone, giving herself a little time for self-study, was an excellent compromise.

She'd been born in the squat two-story cabin behind her, and she'd spent the first five years of her life here in these mountains, living as free and unfettered as a deer.

It made her smile to remember how she and her younger sister had run barefoot, how they had believed the world began and ended with them and their counterculture parents.

She could still picture her mother weaving mats and rugs and her father digging happily in his garden. At night there had been music and long, fascinating stories. The four of them had been happily self-sufficient, seeing other people only on their monthly trips to Brookings for supplies.

They might have continued just that way, but the sixties had become the seventies. An art dealer had discovered one of Libby's mother's wall hangings. Almost simultaneously her father had found that a certain mixture of his homegrown herbs brewed into a soothing and delicious tea. Before Libby's eighth birthday her mother had become a respected artist and her father a successful young entrepreneur. The cabin had become a vacation hideaway when the family had moved into the Portland mainstream.

Perhaps it was Libby's own culture shock that had steered her toward anthropology. Her fascination with it, with society's structures and the effects of outside influences, had often dominated her life. Sometimes she nearly forgot the times she was living in with her avid quest for answers. Whenever that happened she came back here or took a few days to visit her family. That was all it took to ground her in the present.

Starting tomorrow, she decided, if the storm was over, she would turn her computer on and get to work. But only for four hours a day. For the past eighteen months she had too often worked triple that.

Everything in its time—that was what her mother had always said. Well, this time she was going to get back a little of the freedom she'd experienced during the first five years of her life.

Peaceful. Libby let the wind rush through her hair and listened to the hammering of rain on rock and earth. Despite the storm and the rocketing thunder, she felt serene. In all her life she had never known a more peaceful spot.

She saw the light race across the sky, and for a moment she was fooled into thinking it might be ball lightning, or perhaps a meteor. But when the sky lit up she caught a vague outline and a quick flash of metal. She stepped forward, into the rain, instinctively narrowing her eyes. As the object rushed closer, she raised her hand to her throat.

A plane? Even as she watched, it seemed to skim the tops of the firs just to the west of the cabin. The crash echoed through the woods, leaving her frozen to the spot. Then she was running back into the cabin for her slicker and her first-aid kit.

Moments later, with the thunder rolling overhead, she clambered into her Land Rover. She'd noted the spot where she'd seen the plane go down, and she could only hope her sense of direction was as keen as it had always been.

It took her almost thirty minutes of fighting both the blinding storm and the rain-rutted roads and logging trails. She gritted her teeth as the Land Rover plunged through a swollen stream. She knew all too well the dangers of flash floods in the mountains. Still, she kept her speed just above the point of safety, negotiating the twists and turns as much from instinct as from memory. As it happened, she almost ran over him.

Libby hit the brakes hard when her headlights beamed over a figure crumpled at the side of the narrow trail. The Land Rover skidded, spitting mud, before the wheels grabbed hold. Grabbing her flashlight, she scrambled out to kneel beside him.

Alive. She felt a surge of relief when she pressed her fingers against the pulse in his throat. He was dressed all in black, and he was already soaked to the skin. Automatically she tossed the blanket she was carrying over him and began to probe for broken bones.

He was young and lean and well muscled. As she examined him she prayed that those facts would work in his favor. Ignoring the lightning racing across the sky, she played her flashlight over his face.

The gash on his forehead concerned her. Even in the driving rain she could see that it was bleeding badly, but the possibility of a broken back or neck made her reluctant to shift him. Moving quickly, she went back for the first-aid kit. She was applying a butterfly bandage to his wound when he opened his eyes.

Thank God. That single thought ran through her mind as she instinctively took his hand to soothe him. "You're going to be all right. Don't worry. Are you alone?"

He stared at her but saw only a vague outline. "What?"

"Was there anyone with you? Is anyone else hurt?"

"No." He struggled to sit up. The world spun again as he grabbed at her for support. His hands slid off her wet slicker. "I'm alone," he managed before he blacked out again.

He had no idea just how alone.

* * *

Libby slept in snatches most of the night. She'd been able to get him inside the cabin and as far as the couch. She'd stripped him, dried him and tended his wounds before she'd fallen into a half doze in the big armchair by the fire. Periodically, she rose to check his pulse and pupils.

He was in shock, and she'd decided he undoubtedly had a concussion, but the rest of his wounds were relatively minor. Some bruised ribs and a few nasty scratches. A very lucky man, she mused as she sipped her tea and studied him in the firelight. Most fools were. Who else but a fool would have been flying through the mountains in a storm like this?

It was still raging outside the cabin. She set the cup aside to throw another log on the fire. The light grew, sending towering shadows throughout the room. A very attractive fool, she added with a smile as she arched her sore back. He was an inch or two over six feet, and well built. She considered it good luck for both of them that she was strong, accustomed to carrying heavy packs and equipment. Leaning against the mantel, she watched him.

Definitely attractive, she thought again. He'd be even more so when his color returned. Though he was pale now, his face had good bone structure. Celtic, she thought, with those lean, high cheekbones and that full, sculpted mouth. It was a face that hadn't seen a razor for a day or two. That and the bandage on his forehead gave him a rakish, almost dangerous look. His eyes were blue, she remembered, a particularly dark, intense blue.

Definitely Celtic origins, she thought again as she picked up her tea. His hair was black, coal black, and it waved slightly even when it was dry. He wore it too long to be military, she reflected, frowning as she remembered the clothes she'd taken off him. The black jumpsuit had a decidedly military look to it, and there had been some sort of insignia over the breast pocket. Perhaps he was in some elite section of the air force.

She shrugged and settled into the chair. Then again, he'd worn old, scuffed high-top sneakers, as well. Sneakers, and a very expensive-looking watch—one with a half-dozen tiny dials. The only thing she'd been able to figure out on it after a brief look was that it wasn't keeping the right time. Apparently both the watch and its owner had been damaged in the crash.

"I don't know about the watch," she told him over a yawn, "but I think you're going to be all right." With that she dozed off again.

He woke once with a splitting headache and blurred vision. There was firelight, or a first-class simulation. He could smell the woodsmoke…and rain, he thought.

He had a misty memory of having stumbled through the rain. The most he could concentrate on was the fact that he was alive. And warm. He remembered being cold and wet and disoriented, afraid at first that he had crashed into an ocean. There had been…someone. A woman. Low, quiet voice…soft, gentle hands… He tried to think, but the drumming in his head made the effort too painful.

He saw her sitting in an old chair with a colorful blanket over her lap. A hallucination? Maybe, but it was certainly a pleasant one. Her hair was dark, and the fire-light was glinting off it. It appeared to be chin-length and very full and was now tousled appealingly around her face. She was sleeping. He could see the quiet rise and fall of her breasts. In this light her skin seemed to glow gold. Her features were sharp, almost exotic, set off by a wide mouth that was soft and relaxed in sleep.

As hallucinations went, you couldn't do much better.

Closing his eyes again, he slept until sunrise.

She was gone when he surfaced the second time. The fire was still crackling, and the dim light coming through the window was watery. The pain in his head hadn't dulled, but it was bearable. With cautious fingertips he probed the bandage on his forehead. He realized he might have been unconscious for hours or for days. Even as he tried to struggle upright, he discovered that his body was weak and rubbery.

So was his mind, obviously, he decided as he used what strength he had to take in his surroundings. The small, dimly lit room appeared to be fashioned out of stone and wood. He'd seen some carefully preserved relics that had been built of such primitive materials. His family had once taken a vacation west that had included tours of parks and monuments. He turned his head enough so that he could watch the flames eat at the logs. The heat was dry, and the scent was smoke. But it was hardly likely that he would have been given shelter and care in a museum or a historical park.

The worst part was that he didn't have a clue where he was.

"Oh, you're awake." Libby paused in the doorway with a cup of tea in her hand. When her patient just stared at her, she smiled reassuringly and crossed to the couch. He looked so helpless that the shyness she had battled all her life was easily overcome. "I've been worried about you." She sat on the edge of the couch and took his pulse.

He could see her more clearly now. Her hair was no longer tousled, but was combed sleekly from a side part. It was a warm shade of brown. *Exotic* was exactly the right word to describe her, he decided, with her long-lidded eyes, slender nose and full mouth. In profile she reminded him of a drawing he'd once seen of the ancient Egyptian queen Cleopatra. The fingers that lay lightly on his wrist were cool.

"Who are you?"

Steady, she thought with a nod as she continued to monitor his pulse. And stronger. "I'm not Florence Nightingale, but I'm all you've got." She smiled again and, holding each of his eyelids up in turn, peered closely at his pupils. "How many of me do you see?"

"How many should I see?"

With a chuckle, she arranged a pillow behind his back. "Just one, but since you're concussed, you may be seeing twins."

"I only see one." Smiling, he reached up to touch her subtly pointed chin. "One beautiful one."

Color rushed into her cheeks even as she jerked her head back. She wasn't used to being called beautiful, only competent. "Try some of this. My father's secret blend. It isn't even on the market yet."

Before he could decline, she was holding the cup to his lips. "Thanks." Oddly, the flavor brought back a foggy memory of childhood. "What am I doing here?"

"Recovering. You crashed your plane in the mountains a few miles from here."

"My plane?"

"Don't you remember?" A frown came and went in her eyes. Gold eyes. Big, tawny gold eyes. "It'll come back after a bit, I imagine. You took a bad hit on the head." She urged more tea on him and resisted a foolish urge to brush the hair back from his forehead. "I was watching the storm, or I might not have seen you go down. It's fortunate you're not hurt more than you are. There's no phone in the cabin, and the two-way's in being repaired, so I can't even call for a doctor."

"Two-way?"

"The radio," she said gently. "Do you think you could eat?"

"Maybe. Your name?"

"Liberty Stone." She set the tea aside, then laid a hand on his brow to check for fever. She considered it a minor miracle that he hadn't caught a chill. "My parents were in the first wave of sixties counterculture. So I'm Liberty, which is better than my sister, who got stuck with Sunbeam." Noting his confusion, she laughed. "Just call me Libby. How about you?"

"I don't—" The hand on his brow was cool and real. So she had to be real, he reasoned. But what in the hell was she talking about?

"What's your name? I usually like to know who it is I've saved from plane wrecks."

He opened his mouth to tell her—and his mind was blank. Panic skidded along his spine. She saw it whiten his face and glaze his eyes before his fingers clamped hard over her wrist. "I can't—I can't remember."

"Don't push it." She swore silently, thinking of the

radio she had so conscientiously taken for repairs on her trip in for supplies. "You're disoriented. I want you to rest, try to relax, and I'll fix you something to eat."

When he closed his eyes, she got directly to her feet and started back into the kitchen. He'd had no identification, Libby remembered as she began to prepare an omelet. No wallet, no papers, no permits. He could be anyone. A criminal, a psychopath… No. Laughing to herself, she grated some cheese over the egg mixture. Her imagination had always been fruitful. Hadn't the ability to picture primitive and ancient cultures as real people—families, lovers, children—pushed her forward in her career?

But, imagination aside, she had also always been a good judge of character. That, too, probably came from her fascination with people and their habits. And, she admitted ruefully, from the fact that she had always been more comfortable observing people than interacting with them.

The man who was wrestling with his own demons in her living room wasn't a threat to her. Whoever he was, he was harmless. She flipped the omelet expertly, then turned to reach for a plate. With a shriek, she dropped the pan, eggs and all. Her harmless patient was standing, gloriously naked, in her kitchen doorway.

"Hornblower," he managed as he started to slide down the jamb. "Caleb Hornblower."

Dimly he heard her swearing at him. Shaking off his giddiness, he surfaced to find her face close to his. Her arms were around him, and she was struggling to drag him up. In an attempt to help her, he reached out and sent them both sprawling.

Winded, Libby lay flat on her back, pinned under his body. "You'd better still be disoriented."

"Sorry." He had time to register that she was tall and very firm. "Did I knock you down?"

"Yes." Her arms were still around him, her hands splayed over a ridge of muscle along his back. She snatched them away, blaming her breathlessness on her fall. "Now, if you don't mind, you're a little heavy."

He managed to brace one hand on the floor and push himself up a couple of inches. He was dazed, he admitted to himself, but he wasn't dead. And she felt like heaven beneath him. "Maybe I'm too weak to move."

Was that amusement? Yes, Libby decided, that was definitely amusement in his eyes. That ageless and particularly infuriating male amusement. "Hornblower, if you don't move, you're going to be a whole lot weaker." She caught the quick flash of his grin before she squirmed out from under him. She made a halfhearted attempt to keep her eyes on his face—and only his face—as she helped him up. "If you're going to walk around, you're going to have to wait until you can manage it on your own." She slipped a supporting hand around his waist and instantly felt a strong, uncomfortable reaction. "And until I dig through my father's things and find you some pants."

"Right." He sank gratefully onto the couch.

"This time stay put until I come back."

He didn't argue. He couldn't. The walk to the kitchen doorway and back had sapped what strength he'd had left. It was an odd and unwelcome feeling, this weakness. He couldn't remember having been sick a day in his adult life. True, he'd bashed himself up pretty good in that aircycle wreck, but he'd been, what—eighteen?

Damn it, if he could remember that, why couldn't he remember how he'd gotten here? Closing his eyes, he sat back and tried to think above the throbbing in his head.

He'd wrecked his plane. That was what she—Libby— had said. He certainly felt as though he'd wrecked something. It would come back, just as his name had come back to him after that initial terrifying blankness.

She walked back in carrying a plate. "Lucky for you I just laid in supplies." When he opened his eyes, she hesitated and nearly bobbled the eggs a second time. The way he looked, she told herself, half-naked, with only a blanket tossed over his lap and the glow of the fire dancing over his skin, was enough to make any woman's hands unsteady. Then he smiled.

"It smells good."

"My specialty." She let out a long, quiet breath, then sat beside him. "Can you manage it?"

"Yeah. I only get dizzy when I stand up." He took the plate and let his hunger hold sway. After the first bite, he sent her a surprised glance. "Are these real?"

"Real? Of course they're real."

With a little laugh, he took another forkful. "I haven't had real eggs in—I don't remember."

She thought she'd read somewhere that the military used egg substitutes. "These are real eggs from real chickens." The way he plowed his way through them made her smile. "You can have more."

"This should hold me." He looked back to see her smiling as she sipped her ever-present cup of tea. "I guess I haven't thanked you for helping me out."

"I just happened to be in the right place at the right time."

"Why are you here?" He took another look around the cabin. "In this place?"

"I suppose you could say I'm on sabbatical. I'm a cultural anthropologist, and I've just finished several months of field research. I'm working on my dissertation."

"Here?"

It pleased her that he hadn't made the usual comment about her being too young to be a scientist. "Why not?" She took his empty plate and set it aside. "It's quiet—except for the occasional plane crash. How are your ribs? Hurt?"

He looked down, noticing the bruises for the first time. "No, not really. Just sore."

"You know, you're very lucky. Except for the head wound, you got out of that with cuts and bruises. The way you were coming down, I didn't expect to find anyone alive."

"The crash control…" He got a misty image of himself pushing switches. Lights, flashing lights. The echo of warning bells. He tried to focus, to concentrate, but it broke apart.

"Are you a test pilot?"

"What? No… No, I don't think so."

She put a comforting hand on his. Then, unnerved by the depth of her reaction, cautiously removed it again.

"I don't like puzzles," he muttered.

"I'm crazy about them. So I'll help you put this one together."

He turned his head until their eyes met. "Maybe you won't like the solution."

A ripple of unease ran through her. He'd be strong. When his injuries healed, his body would be as strong as she sensed his mind was. And they were alone…as completely alone as any two people could be. She shook off the feeling and busied herself drinking tea. What was she supposed to do, toss him and his concussion out into the rain?

"We won't know until we find it," she said at length. "If the storm lets up, I should be able to get you to a doctor in a day or two. In the meantime, you'll have to trust me."

He did. He couldn't have said why, but from the moment he'd seen her dozing in the chair he'd known she was someone he could count on. The problem was, he didn't know if he could trust himself—or if she could.

"Libby…" She turned toward him again, and the moment she did he lost what he'd wanted to say. "You have a nice face," he murmured, and watched her tawny eyes turn wary. He wanted to touch her, felt compelled to. But the moment he lifted his hand she was up and out of reach.

"I think you should get some more rest. There's a spare bedroom upstairs." She was speaking quickly now, her words fast and edgy. "I couldn't get you up there last night, but you'd be more comfortable."

He studied her for a moment. He wasn't used to women backing away from him. Cal mused over that impression until he was certain it was a true one. No, when there was attraction between a man and a woman, the rest was easy. Maybe all his circuits weren't working, but he knew there was attraction on both sides.

"Are you matched?"

Libby's brows lifted into her fringe of bangs. "Am I what?"

"Matched? Do you have a mate?"

She had to laugh. "That's a quaint way of putting it. No, not at the moment. Let me help you upstairs." She held up a hand before he could push himself up. "I'd really appreciate it if you'd keep that blanket on."

"It's not cold," he said. Then, with a shrug, he hooked the material around his hips.

"Here, lean on me." She draped his arm over her shoulder, then slipped her own around his waist. "Steady?"

"Almost." When they started forward, he found that he was only slightly dizzy. He was almost sure he could have made it on his own, but he liked the idea of starting up the stairs with his arm wrapped around her. "I've never been in a place like this before."

Her heart was beating a little too quickly. Since he was putting almost none of his weight on her, she couldn't blame it on exertion. Proximity, however, was a different matter. "I suppose it's rustic by most standards, but I've always loved it."

Rustic was a mild word for it, he mused, but he didn't want to offend her. "Always?"

"Yes, I was born here."

He started to speak again, but when he turned his

head he caught a whiff of her hair. When his body tightened, he became aware of his bruises.

"Right in here. Sit at the foot of the bed while I turn it down." He did as she asked, then ran his hand over one of the bedposts, amazed. It was wood, he was certain it was wood, but it didn't seem to be more than twenty or thirty years old. And that was ridiculous.

"This bed…"

"It's comfortable, really. Dad made it, so it's a little wobbly, but the mattress is good."

Cal's fingers tightened on the post. "Your father made this? It's wood?"

"Solid oak, and heavy as a truck. Believe it or not, I was born in it, since at that time my parents didn't believe in doctors for something as basic and personal as childbirth. I still find it hard to picture my father with his hair in a ponytail and wearing love beads." She straightened and caught Cal staring at her. "Is something wrong?"

He just shook his head. He must need rest—a lot more rest. "Was this—" He made a weak gesture to indicate the cabin. "Was this some kind of experiment?"

Her eyes softened, showing a combination of amusement and affection. "You could call it that." She went to a rickety bureau her father had built. After rummaging through it, she came up with a pair of sweatpants.

"You can wear these. Dad always leaves some clothes out here, and you're pretty much the same size."

"Sure." He took her hand before she could leave the room. "Where did you say we were?"

He looked so concerned that she covered his hand with hers. "Oregon, southwest Oregon, just over the California border in the Klamath Mountains."

"Oregon." The tension in his fingers relaxed slightly. "U.S.A.?"

"The last time I looked." Concerned, she checked for fever again.

He took her wrist, concentrating on keeping his grip light. "What planet?"

Her eyes flew to his. If she hadn't known better, she would have sworn the man was serious. "Earth. You know, the third from the sun," she said, humoring him. "Get some rest, Hornblower. You're just rattled."

"Yeah." He let out a long breath. "I guess you're right."

"Just yell if you need something."

He sat where he was when she left him. He had a feeling, a bad one. But she was probably right—he was rattled. If he was in Oregon, in the northern hemisphere of his own planet, he wasn't that far off course. Off course, he repeated as his head began to pound. What course had he been on?

He looked down at the watch on his wrist and

frowned at the dials. In a gesture that came from instinct rather than thought, he pressed the small stem on the side. The dials faded, and a series of red numbers blinked on the black face.

Los Angeles. A wave of relief washed over him as he recognized the coordinates. He'd been returning to base in L.A. after...after what, damn it?

He lay down slowly and discovered that Libby had been right. The bed was surprisingly comfortable. Maybe if he just went to sleep, clocked out for a few hours, he would remember the rest. Because it seemed important to her, Cal tugged on the sweats.

What had she gotten herself into? Libby wondered. She sat in front of her computer and stared at the blank screen. She had a sick man on her hands—an incredibly good-looking sick man. One with a concussion, partial amnesia...and eyes to die for. She sighed and propped her chin on her hands. The concussion she could handle. She'd considered learning extensive first aid as important as studying the tribal habits of Western man. Fieldwork often took scientists to remote places where doctors and hospitals didn't exist.

But her training didn't help her with the amnesia. And it certainly didn't help her with his eyes. Her knowledge of man came straight out of books and usually dealt with his cultural and sociopolitical habits. Any one-on-one had been purely scientific research.

She could put up a good front when it was necessary. Her battle with a crushing shyness had been long and hard. Ambition had pushed her through, driving her to ask questions when she would have preferred to have melded with the background and been ignored. It had given her the strength to travel, to work with strangers, to make a select few trusted friends.

But when it came to a personal man-woman relationship…

For the most part, the men she saw socially were easily dissuaded. The majority of them were intimidated by her mind, which she admitted was usually one-track. Then there was her family. Thinking of them made her smile. Her mother was still the dreamy artist who had once woven blankets on a handmade loom. And her father… Libby shook her head as she thought of him. William Stone might have made a fortune with Herbal Delight, but he would never be a three-piece-suit executive.

Bob Dylan music and board meetings. Lost causes and profit margins.

The one man she'd brought home to a family dinner had left confused and unnerved—and undoubtedly hungry, Libby remembered with a laugh. He hadn't

been able to do more than stare at her mother's zuc-
chini-and-soybean soufflé.

Libby was a combination of her parents' idealism,
scientific practicality and dreamy romanticism. She
believed in causes, in mathematical equations and in
fairy tales. A quick mind and a thirst for knowledge
had locked her far too tightly to her work to leave room
for real romance. And the truth was that real romance,
when applied to her, scared the devil out of her.

So she sought it in the past, in the study of human
relationships.

She was twenty-three and, as Caleb Hornblower had
put it, unmatched.

She liked the phrase, found it accurate and concise
on the one hand and highly romantic on the other. To be
matched, she mused, was the perfect way to describe a
relationship. She corrected herself. A true relationship,
like her parents'. Perhaps the reason she was more at
ease with her studies than with men was that she had
yet to meet her match.

Satisfied with her analysis, she slipped on her glasses
and went to work.

Chapter 2

The rain had slowed when he woke. It was only a hiss and patter against the windows. It was as soothing as a sleep tape. Cal lay still for a moment, reminding himself where he was and struggling to remember why.

He'd dreamed...something about flashing lights and a huge black void. The dreams had brought a clammy sweat to his skin and had accelerated his heartbeat. He made a conscious effort to level it.

Pilots had to have a strong and thorough control over their bodies and their emotions. Decisions often had to be made instantly, even instinctively. And the rigors of flight required a disciplined, healthy body.

He was a pilot. He kept his eyes closed and concentrated on that. He'd always wanted to fly. He'd been trained. His mouth went dry as he fought to remember…anything, any small piece.

The ISF. He closed his hands into fists until his pulse leveled again. He'd been with the ISF and earned a captaincy. Captain Hornblower. That was right, he was sure of it. Captain Caleb Hornblower. Cal. Everyone called him Cal except his mother. A tall, striking woman with a quick temper and an easy laugh.

A new flood of emotion struck him. He could see her. Somehow that, more than anything else, gave him a sense of identity. He had family—not a mate, of that he was sure, but parents and a brother. His father was a quiet man, steady, dependable. His brother…Jacob. Cal let out a quiet breath as the name and the image formed in his mind. Jacob was brilliant, impulsive, stubborn.

Because his head was pounding again, he let it go. It was enough.

His eyes opened slowly and he thought of Libby. Who was she? Not just a beautiful woman with warm brown hair and eyes like a cat. Being beautiful was easy, even ordinary. She didn't strike him as ordinary. Perhaps it was the place. He frowned at the log walls and the gleaming glass windows. Nothing was ordinary here. And certainly no woman he had ever known would have chosen to live here, like this. Alone.

Had she really been born in the bed he was now in, or had she been joking? It occurred to Cal that a great deal of her behavior was odd, and perhaps there was a joke somewhere, and he'd missed the punch line.

A cultural anthropologist, he mused. That might explain it. It was possible he'd dropped down in the middle of some kind of field experiment, a simulation. For her own reasons, Liberty Stone was living in the fashion of the era she studied. It was odd, certainly, but as far as he was concerned most scientists were a bit odd. He could certainly understand looking toward the future, but why anyone would want to dig back into the past was beyond him. The past was done and couldn't be changed or fixed, so why study it?

Her business, he supposed.

He owed her. From what he could piece together, he might well have died if she hadn't come along. He'd have to pay her back as soon as he was working on all thrusters again. It pleased him to know that he was a man who settled debts.

Liberty Stone. Libby. He turned her name over in his mind and smiled. He liked the sound of her name, the soft sound of it. Soft, like her eyes. It was one thing to be beautiful; it was another to have gorgeous velvet eyes. You could change the color of them, the shape, but never the expression. Maybe it was that that made her so appealing. Everything she felt seemed to leap right into her eyes.

He'd managed to stir a variety of feelings in her, Cal

thought as he pushed himself up in bed. Concern, fear, humor, desire. And she had stirred him. Even through his confusion he'd felt a strong, healthy response, a man-woman response.

He dropped his head into his hands as the room spun. His system might be churning for Libby Stone, but he was far from ready to do anything about it. More than a little disgusted, he settled back on the pillows. A little more rest, he decided. A day or two of letting his body heal should snap his mind and his memory back. He knew who he was and where he was. The rest would come.

A book on the table beside the bed caught his eye. He'd always liked to read, almost as much as he'd liked to fly. He preferred the written word to tapes or disks. That was another good and solid memory. Pleased with it, Cal picked up the book.

The title puzzled him. *Journey to Andromeda* seemed a particularly foolish name for a book, especially when it was touted as science fiction. Anyone with a free weekend could journey to Andromeda—if he liked being bored into a coma. With a small frown, he started to leaf through the book. Then his eyes fell on the copyright page.

That was wrong. The clammy sweat was back. That was ridiculous. The book he was holding was new. The back hadn't been broken, and the pages looked as though they'd never been turned. Some stupid clerical error, he told himself, but his mouth was bone-dry. It had to be an error. How else could he be holding a book that had been published nearly three centuries ago?

Absorbed in her work, Libby ignored the small circle of pain at the center of her back. She knew very well that posture was important when she was writing for several hours at a stretch, but once she lost herself in ancient or primitive civilizations she always forgot everything else.

She hadn't eaten since breakfast, and the tea she'd carried up with her was stone-cold. Her notes and reference books were scattered everywhere, along with clothes she hadn't yet put away and the stack of newspapers she'd picked up at the store. She'd toed off her shoes and had her stockinged feet curled around the legs of her chair. Occasionally she stopped hammering at the keyboard to push her round, black-framed glasses back on her nose.

It cannot be argued that the addition of modern implements has a strong and not always positive effect on an isolated culture such as the Kolbari. The islanders have remained, in the latter years of the twentieth century, at a folk level and do not, as has been implied in the human relations area files, seek integration with the modern industrial societies. What may be seen by certain factions as offering the convenience of progress, medically, industrially, educationally, is most often—

"Libby."

"What?" The word came out in a hiss of annoyance before she turned. "Oh." She spotted Cal, pale and shaky, with one hand braced on the door frame and the other wrapped around a paperback. "What are you doing up, Hornblower? I told you to call if you needed anything." Annoyed with him and with the interruption, she rose to help him to a chair. The moment she touched his arm, he jerked away.

"What are you wearing on your face?"

The tone of his voice had her moistening her lips. It was fury, with a touch of fear. A dangerous combination. "Glasses. Reading glasses."

"I know what they are, damn it. Why are you wearing them?"

Go slow, she warned herself. She took his arm gently and spoke as if she were soothing a wounded lion. "I need them to work."

"Why haven't you had them fixed?"

"My glasses?"

He gritted his teeth. "Your eyes. Why haven't you had your eyes fixed?"

Cautious, she took the glasses off and held them behind her back. "Why don't you sit down?"

He only shook his head. "I want to know the meaning of this."

Libby looked at the book in his hand, the one he was shaking in her face. She cleared her throat. "I don't know the meaning, since I haven't read it. I imagine my father left it here. He's into science fiction."

"That's not what I—" Patience, he told himself. He had never had an abundance of it, and now was the time to use all he could find. "Open it up to the copyright page."

"All right. I will if you'll sit. You're not looking well."

He reached the chair in two rocky strides. "Open it. Read the date."

Head injuries could often cause erratic behavior, Libby thought. She didn't believe he was dangerous, but all the same she decided it was best to humor him and read the year out loud, then she tried an easy smile. "Hot off the presses," she added.

"Is that supposed to be a joke?"

"I'm not sure." He was furious, she realized. And terrified. "Caleb." She said his name quietly as she crouched beside him.

"Does that book have something to do with your work?"

"My work?" The question threw her off enough to have her frowning at him, then at the computer behind her. "I'm an anthropologist. That means I study—"

"I know what it means." Patience be damned, he thought. Incensed, he snatched the book from her. "I want to know what this means."

"It's just a book. If I know my father, it's second-rate science fiction about invasions from the planet Kriswold. You know, mutants and ray guns and space warriors. That kind of thing." She eased it from his hand. "Let me get you back to bed. I'll make you some soup."

He looked at her, saw the soft eyes overflowing with concern, the encouraging half smile. And the nerves. His gaze shifted to where her hand lay almost protectively over his, despite the fact that he had obviously frightened her. There was a link there. It was absurd to believe that, almost as absurd as it was to believe the date in the book.

"Maybe I'm losing my mind."

"No." Her fear forgotten, she lifted her free hand to his face, soothing him as she would have anyone who seemed so utterly lost. "You're hurt."

He closed surprisingly strong fingers over her wrist. "Jolted the memory banks? Yeah, maybe. Libby…" His eyes were suddenly intense, almost desperate. "What's the date today?"

"It's May the 24th or 25th. I lose track."

"No, the whole thing." He fought to keep the urgency out of his voice. "Please."

"Okay, it's probably Tuesday, the 25th." Then she repeated the year. "How's that?"

"Fine." He pulled out every ounce of control and managed to smile at her. One of them was crazy, and he dearly hoped it was Libby. "You got anything to drink around here besides that tea?"

She frowned for a moment. Then her face cleared. "Brandy. There's always some downstairs. Hold on a minute."

"Yeah, thanks."

He waited until he heard her moving down the stairs. Then, cautiously, he rose and pulled open the first drawer that came to hand. There had to be something in this ridiculous place to tell him what was going on.

He found lingerie, neatly stacked despite the chaos of the rest of the room. He frowned a moment over the styles and materials. She'd said she wasn't matched, yet it was obvious that she wore things to please a man. Apparently she preferred the romance of past eras even when it came to her underwear. Far from comfortable with the ease with which he could picture Libby in this little chocolate-brown swatch with the white lace, he shoved the drawer shut again.

The next drawer was just as tidy and held jeans and sturdy hiking pants. He puzzled for a moment over a zipper, ran it slowly up and down, then shoved the jeans back into place. Annoyed, he turned and started toward her desk, where her computer continued to hum. He had time to think it was a noisy, archaic machine before he stumbled over the pile of newspapers. He didn't scan the headlines or study the picture. His eyes were drawn to the date.

He was unarguably in the twentieth century.

His stomach clenched. Ignoring the sudden buzzing in his ears, he bent to snatch up the paper. Words danced in front of his eyes. Something about arms talks—nuclear arms, he noted with a kind of dull horror—and hail damage in the Midwest. There was a tease about the Mariners trouncing the Braves. Very slowly, knowing his legs would give out in a moment, he lowered himself back into the chair.

It was too bad, he thought dully. It was too damn bad, but it wasn't Libby Stone who was going crazy.

"Caleb?" The moment she saw his face, Libby rushed into the room with brandy sloshing in a snifter. "You're white as a sheet."

"It's nothing." He had to be careful now, very careful. "I guess I stood up too fast."

"I think you really could use some of this." She held the snifter until she was certain he had both hands on it. "Take it slow," she began, but he'd already drained it. Sitting back on her heels, she frowned at him. "That should cure you or knock you out again."

The brandy was the genuine article and no hallucination, he decided. It was velvet fire coursing down his throat. He closed his eyes and let the fire spread. "I'm still a little disoriented. How long have I been here?"

"Since last night." The color was coming back, she noted. His voice sounded calmer, more controlled. It wasn't until her muscles relaxed that she realized how tightly they'd been tensed. "I guess I saw you crash about midnight."

"You saw it?"

"Well, I saw the lights and heard you hit." She smiled, continuing to monitor his pulse, when he opened his eyes again. "For a minute I thought I was seeing a meteor or a UFO or something."

"A—a UFO?" he repeated, dazed.

"Not that I believe in extraterrestrials or spaceships or anything, but my father's always been fascinated by that kind of thing. I realized it was a plane." He was staring at her again, she thought, but there was curiosity rather than anger in his eyes. "Feeling better?"

He couldn't have begun to tell her how and what he was feeling. Cal had an idea that that was all for the best. He needed to think before he said too much. "Some." Still hoping it was all some bizarre mistake, he rattled the paper in his hand. "Where'd you get this?"

"I drove into Brookings a couple of days ago. That's about seventy miles from here. I picked up supplies and a few newspapers." She glanced absently at the one in his hand. "I haven't gotten around to reading any of them yet, so they're already old news."

"Yeah." He looked at the papers that were still on the floor. "Old news."

With a laugh, she rose and began to make an effort to tidy the room. "I always feel so cut off here, more so than when I'm in the field hundreds of miles away. I imagine we could establish a colony on Mars and I wouldn't hear about it until it was all over."

"A colony on Mars," he murmured, feeling his stomach sink as he glanced at the paper again. "I think you've got about a hundred years to go."

"Sorry I'll miss it." With a sigh, she looked out the window. "Rain's starting up again. Maybe we can catch the weather on the early news." After stepping over books, she flicked on a small portable television. After a moment, a snowy picture blinked on. She dragged a hand through her hair and decided to watch without her glasses. "The weather should be on in a—Caleb?" She tilted her head to one side, fascinated by his dumbstruck expression. "I'd swear you'd never seen a television in your life."

"What?" He brought himself back, wishing he had another brandy. A television. He'd heard of them, of course, in the same way Libby had heard of covered wagons. "I didn't realize you had one."

"We're rustic," she told him, "not primitive." She narrowed her eyes when he gave a choked laugh. "Maybe you should lie down again."

"Yeah." And when he woke up again, this would all have been a dream. "Mind if I take these papers?"

She stood to help him up. "I don't know if you should be reading."

"I think that's the least of my worries." He discovered that the room didn't spin this time, but it was still a comfort to drape his arm around her shoulders. Strong shoulders, he thought. And a soft scent. "Libby, if I wake up and find out this has all been an illusion, I want you to know you've been the best part of it."

"That's nice."

"I mean it." The brandy and his own weakened system were taking over. Because his mind felt as if it had been fried in a solar blast, he didn't fight it. She had little trouble easing him into bed. But his arm stayed around her shoulders long enough to keep her close, just close enough to brush his lips over hers. "The very best."

She jerked back like a spring. He was asleep, and her blood was pounding.

Who was Caleb Hornblower? The question interrupted Libby's work throughout the evening. Her interest in the Kolbari Islanders didn't even come close to her growing fascination with her unexpected and confusing guest.

Who was he, and what was she going to do about him? The trouble was, she had a whole list of unanswered questions that applied to her odd patient, Caleb Hornblower. Libby was a great listmaker, and a woman who knew herself well enough to be aware that all her organizational talents were eaten up by her work.

Who was he? Why had he been flying through a storm at midnight? Where did he come from and where had he been going? Why had a simple paperback novel sent him into a panic? Why had he kissed her?

Libby pulled herself up short there. That particular question wasn't important—it wasn't even relevant. He hadn't really kissed her, she reminded herself. And whether he had or hadn't wasn't the issue. It was gratitude, she decided, and began to nibble on her thumbnail. He'd only been trying to show her that he was grateful to her. Libby certainly understood that a kiss was—could be—a very casual gesture. It was part of Western culture. Over the centuries it had become as unimportant as a smile or a handshake. It was a sign of friendship, affection, sympathy, gratitude. And desire. She bit down harder on her nail.

Not all societies used the kiss, of course. Many tribal cultures… She was lecturing again, Libby thought in disgust. She looked down at her hands. And she was biting her nails. That was a bad sign.

What she needed was to get her mind off Hornblower for a while and fill her stomach. Pressing a hand to it, Libby rose. She wasn't going to get any work done this way, so she might as well eat.

Since Caleb's room was dark, she passed it by, telling herself she'd check on him when she came back up. Sleep was undoubtedly more essential to his recovery than another meal.

There was a low rumble of thunder as she descended the stairs. Another bad sign, she thought. At this rate it would be days before she could get him down the mountain.

Perhaps someone was already looking for him. Friends, family, business associates. A wife or a lover. Everyone had someone.

She groped for the kitchen light as the sky cracked with the first bolt of lightning. It was going to be another boomer, she decided as she opened the refrigerator door. Finding nothing that appealed to her, she rummaged through the cupboards. A night like this called for a nice bowl of soup and a seat by the fire.

Alone.

She sighed a little as she opened the can. Recently she'd begun to think about being alone. As a scientist she knew the reason. She lived in a culture of couples.

Single—unmatched, she remembered with a quick smile—men and women often found themselves dissatisfied and depressed in their own company. The entertainment media subtly—and not so subtly—drilled into them the pleasures of relationships. Families added pressure for the single to marry and continue the family line. Good-natured friends offered help and advice, generally unwanted, on finding a mate. The human being was programmed, almost from birth, to search for and find a companion of the opposite sex.

Maybe that was why she'd resisted. An interesting analysis, Libby mused as she stirred the soup. The desire for individuality and self-sufficiency had been ingrained in her from birth. It would take a very special person to tempt her to share. She had dated only rarely in high school. The same pattern had held true in college. She'd had no interest.

That wasn't precisely true, she thought. She had had interest—the trouble was, it had usually been scientific. She'd never met a man who dazzled her enough to stop her from making lists and forming hypotheses. Professor Stone, they'd called her in high school. And it still rankled. In college she'd been considered a professional virgin. She'd detested that, had struggled to ignore it, pouring her energy into her studies. The appeal of her personality had made her friends, both male and female. But intimate relationships were another matter.

When all the data had been analyzed, there had never been one who had made her...well, yearn, Libby decided. That was the appropriate term.

She supposed there wasn't a man on the planet who could make her yearn.

Wooden spoon in hand, she turned to take out a bowl. For the second time she saw Cal framed in the doorway. She gave a muffled shriek, and the spoon went flying. A flash of lightning lit up the room. Then it was plunged into darkness.

"Libby?"

"Damn it, Hornblower, I wish you wouldn't do that." Her voice was breathless as she rummaged through drawers for a candle. "You scared the life out of me."

"Did you think I was one of the mutants from Andromeda?" There was a dry tone to the words that had her wrinkling her nose.

"I told you I don't read that stuff." She closed a drawer on her thumb, swore, then wrenched open another. "Where are the stupid matches?" She turned and bumped solidly into his chest in the dark. Lightning flashed again, illuminating his face. It took only that instant for her mouth to go dry. He'd looked stunning, strong and dangerous.

"You're shaking." His voice had gentled almost imperceptibly, but the hands on her shoulders stayed firm. "Are you really frightened?"

"No, I..." She wasn't a woman to be scared of the

dark. Certainly she wasn't a woman to be afraid of a man—intellectually speaking. But she was shaking. The hands that had reached up to his bare chest trembled—and intellect had nothing to do with it. "I need to find the matches."

"Why did you turn the lights off?" She smelled wonderful. In the cool, unrelieved darkness he could concentrate on her scent. It was light and almost sinfully feminine.

"I didn't. The storm knocked out the power." His fingers tightened on her arms, hard enough to make her gasp. "Caleb?"

"Cal." Lightning flashed again, and she saw that his eyes had darkened. He was staring out the window into the storm now. "People call me Cal."

His grip had eased. Though she ordered herself to relax, the crash of the thunder made her jolt. "I like Caleb," she said, hoping her voice was pleasant and casual. "We'll have to save it for special occasions. You have to let me go."

He slid his hands down to her wrists, then back. "Why?"

Her mind went blank. Beneath her palms she could feel the strong, steady beating of his heart. Slowly his fingers skimmed down to her elbows, where his thumbs traced lazy, erotic circles on the sensitive inner skin. She could no longer see him, but she could taste the warm flutter of his breath on her parted lips.

"I…" She felt each separate muscle in her body go lax. "Don't." The word nearly strangled her as she jerked back. "I need to find the matches."

"So you said."

Leaning weakly against the counter, she began to search the drawer again. Even after she found a pack, it took her a full minute to light the match. Thoughtful, his hands plunged deep in the pockets of the sweats, Cal watched the little flame dance and flicker. She lit two tapers, keeping her back to him.

"I was heating soup. Would you like some?"

"All right."

It helped to keep her hands busy. "You must be feeling better."

His mouth twisted into a humorless smile when he thought of the hours he'd lain in the dark willing his memory to return completely. "I must be."

"Headache?"

"Not much of one."

She poured the water she'd already boiled for tea, then arranged everything meticulously on a tray. "I was going to sit by the fire."

"Okay." He picked up the two candles and led the way.

The storm helped, Cal thought. It made everything he was seeing, everything he was doing, seem that much more unreal. Perhaps by the time the rain stopped he'd know what he had to do.

"Did the storm wake you?"

"Yeah." It wouldn't be the last lie he told her. Though he was sorry for the necessity of it, Cal smiled and settled in a chair by the fire. There was something charming about being in a place where a simple rainstorm could leave you in the dark, dependent on candles and firelight. No computer could have set a better scene. "How long do you think it'll be before you regain power?"

"An hour." She tasted the soup. It nearly calmed her. "A day." She laughed and shook her head. "Dad always talked about hooking up a generator, but it was one of those things he never got around to. When we were kids, we'd sometimes have to cook over the fire for days in the winter. And we'd sleep all curled up here on the floor while my parents took turns making sure the fire didn't die out."

"You liked it." Cal knew people who went into preserved areas and camped. He'd always thought they were strange. But the way Libby spoke of it, it seemed homey.

"I loved it. I guess those first five years helped me handle the more primitive parts of digs and fieldwork."

She was relaxed again. He could see it in her eyes, hear it in her voice. Though a nervous Libby held a definite appeal for him, he wanted her relaxed now. The more at ease she was, the more information he might glean.

"What era do you study?"

"No specific era. I'm hung up on tribal life, mainly isolated cultures and the effects of modern tools and machines. Things like how electricity changes the sociopolitical mores of the traditional man. I've toyed around with extinct cultures, Aztecs, Incas." This was easy, she decided. The more she talked about her work, the less she would think about that jolting moment in the kitchen and her own inexplicable reaction to it. "I'm planning on going to Peru in the fall."

"How'd you get started?"

"I think it was a trip to the Yucatan when I was a kid, and all those wonderful Mayan ruins. Have you ever been to Mexico?"

Looking back, he remembered a particularly wild night in Acapulco. "Yes. About ten years ago." Or a couple of centuries from now, he thought, and frowned into his bowl.

"Bad time?"

"What? No. This tea…" He took another sip. "It's familiar."

Grinning, she tucked her legs up under her. "My father will be glad to hear that. Herbal Delight—that's his company. He started it right here in this cabin."

Cal looked down into his cup, then laid his head back and laughed. "I thought that was a myth."

"No." With a half smile forming, she studied him. "I don't get the joke."

"It's hard to explain." Should he tell her that over two centuries from now Herbal Delight would be one of the ten biggest and most powerful companies on Earth and its colonies? Should he tell her that it made not only tea but organic fuel and God knew what else? Here was Cal Hornblower, he thought, sitting cozily in a chair in the cabin where it all began. He noted that she was staring at him as if she were going to check his pulse again.

"My mother used to give me this," he told her. "When I had—" He wasn't sure what childhood illness he could name, but he was certain it wasn't red dust fever. "Whenever I wasn't feeling well."

"A cure for all ills. You're remembering more."

"Patches, pieces," he said, still cautious. "It's easier to remember childhood than last night."

"I don't think that's unusual. Are you married?" Where had that come from? she wondered, and immediately turned her attention to the fire.

He was glad she wasn't looking at him when the grin split his face. "No. It wouldn't be wise for me to want you if I were."

Her mouth dropped open, and she twisted around to

look at him. Quickly she rose and began stacking the dishes on the tray. "I should take these back in."

"Would you rather I didn't tell you?"

She had to swallow once, hard, before she could speak at all. "Tell me what?"

"That I want you." He closed his hand over her wrist to keep her still. It amazed and aroused him to feel her pulse hammering. His word-by-word perusal of the newspaper hadn't given him an inkling of how men and women interacted in the here and now, but he didn't believe it could be so different.

"Yes— No."

Smiling, he took the tray out of her hands. "Which?"

"I don't think it's a good idea." When he stood up, she stepped back and felt the heat from the fire on her legs. "Caleb…"

"Is this a special occasion?" He traced a fingertip across her jaw and watched her eyes go as hot as the flames behind her.

"Don't." It was ridiculous. He couldn't make her tremble with just a touch. But all he had done was touch her. And she was trembling.

"When I woke up and saw you sleeping in the chair in the firelight I thought you were an illusion." He rubbed his thumb gently over her bottom lip. "You look like one now."

She didn't feel like one. She felt real, shatteringly

real, and terrified. "I have to bank the fire for the night, and you should go back to bed."

"We can bank the fire for the night. Then we can go to bed."

She squared her shoulders, furious at the realization that her palms were sweating. She would not stammer, she promised herself. She would not act the inexperienced fool. She would handle him the way a strong, independent woman would, a woman who knew her own mind. "I'm not going to sleep with you. I don't know you."

So that was a condition, Cal mused. After thinking it over, he found it rather sweet and not completely unreasonable. "All right. How long do you need?"

She stared at him. At length she dragged both hands through her hair. "I can't figure out if you're joking or not, but I do know you're the oddest man I've ever met."

"You don't know the half of it." He watched her bank the fire carefully. Competent hands, he thought, an athletic body, and the most vulnerable eyes he'd ever seen. "We'll get to know each other tomorrow. Then we'll sleep together."

She straightened so quickly that she rapped her head on the mantel. Swearing and rubbing her head, she turned to him. "Not necessarily. In fact it's very unlikely."

He took the screen and placed it in front of the fire, exactly as he had seen her do earlier. "Why?"

"Because…" Flustered, she fumbled for words for a moment. "I don't do that kind of thing."

She recognized genuine astonishment when she saw it. It was staring at her now out of Cal's dark blue eyes. "At all?"

"Really, Hornblower, that's none of your business." Dignity helped, but not a great deal. As she swept up the tray, the bowls slid dangerously, and they would have crashed to the floor if he hadn't caught the end of the tray and balanced it.

"Why are you angry? I only want to make love with you."

"Listen." She took a deep breath. "I've had enough of all this. I did you a favor, and I don't appreciate you insinuating that I should hop into bed with you just because you've—you've got an itch. I don't find it flattering—in fact, I find it very insulting—that you think I'd make love with a perfect stranger just because it's convenient."

He tilted his head, trying to take it all in. "Is inconvenient better?"

She could only grit her teeth. "Listen, Hornblower, I'll drop you off at the nearest singles bar the minute we can get out of here. Until then, keep your distance."

With that, she stormed out of the room. He could hear the dishes crash in the kitchen.

He dug his hands in his pockets again as he started upstairs. Twentieth-century women were very difficult to understand. Fascinating, he admitted, but difficult.

And what in the hell was a singles bar?

Chapter 3

He felt almost normal in the morning. Normal, Cal thought, if you considered he hadn't even been born yet. It was a bizarre situation, highly improbable according to most of the current scientific theories, and deep down he clung to the faint hope that he was having some kind of long, involved dream.

If he was lucky, he was in a hospital suffering from shock and a little brain damage. But from the looks of things he'd been snapped back over two centuries into the primitive, often violent twentieth century.

The last thing he could remember before waking up on Libby's couch was flying his ship. No, that wasn't quite accurate. He'd been fighting to fly his ship. Something had happened.... He couldn't quite bring that into focus yet. Whatever it had been, it had been big.

His name was Caleb Hornblower. He'd been born in the year 2222. That made two his lucky number, he remembered with a half laugh. He was thirty, unmatched, the older of two sons, and a former member of the International Space Force. He'd been a captain, and for the last eighteen months he'd been an independent. He'd made a routine supply delivery to the Brigston Colony on Mars and had veered off from his normal route on the return trip home because of a meteor shower. Then it had happened. Whatever *it* was.

Now he had to accept the fact that something had shot him back in time. He had crashed, not only through Earth's atmosphere, but through about two and a half centuries. He was a healthy, intelligent flier who was stuck in a time when people considered interplanetary travel the stuff of science fiction and were, incredibly, playing around with nuclear fission.

The good part was that the experience hadn't killed him and he'd landed in an isolated area in the hands of a gorgeous brunette.

It could, he supposed, be worse.

His problem at the moment was figuring out how he could get back to his own time. Alive.

He adjusted his pillow, scratched at the stubble on

his chin and wondered what Libby's reaction would be if he went downstairs and calmly related his story.

He'd probably find himself out the door, wearing no more than her father's sweats. Or she'd call the authorities and have him hauled off to whatever passed for rest-and-rehabilitation clinics at this point in time. He didn't imagine they were luxury resorts.

What annoyed him at the moment was that he'd been a poor history student. What he knew about the twentieth century would barely fill a computer screen. But he imagined they would have a pretty primitive way of dealing with a man who claimed he'd crashed his F27 into a mountain after making a routine run to Mars.

Until he could find a way out, he was going to have to keep his problem to himself. In order to do so, he'd have to be more careful about what he said. And what he did.

He'd obviously made a misstep the night before. In more ways than one. He grimaced as he recalled Libby's reaction to his simple suggestion that they spend the night together. Things were obviously done differently then—no, now, he corrected. It was a pity he hadn't paid more attention to those old romances his mother liked to read.

In any case, his problems ran a lot deeper than having been rejected by a beautiful woman. He had to get back to his ship, had to try to reconstruct what had happened in his head. Then he had to make it happen in reality. As far as he could see, that was the only way to get home again.

She had a computer, he remembered. As archaic as it was, between that and the mini on his wrist he might be able to calculate a trajectory.

Right now he wanted a shower, a shave and some more of Libby's eggs. He opened his door and nearly walked into her.

The cup of coffee she held was steaming, and she nearly splashed it all over his bare chest. Libby righted it, though she thought a little scalding was just what he deserved.

"I thought you might like some coffee."

"Thanks." He noted that her voice was frigid, her back stiff. Unless he missed his guess, women hadn't changed that much. The cold shoulder never went out of style. "I want to apologize," he began, offering her his best smile. "I know I veered out of orbit last night."

"That's one way of putting it."

"What I mean is…you were right and I was wrong." If that didn't do the trick, he knew nothing about the nature of women.

"All right." Nothing made her more uncomfortable than holding a grudge. "We'll forget it."

"Is it okay if I think you have beautiful eyes?" He saw her blush and was utterly charmed.

"I suppose." The corners of her mouth turned up. She'd been right about the Celtic blood, she reflected. If the man didn't have Irish ancestors, she'd have to go into a different line of work. "If you can't help it."

He held out a hand. "Friends?"

"Friends." The moment she put her hand in his she wondered why it felt as though she'd made a mistake. Or jumped off a bridge. He had a way of using only the barest brush of his fingertips to send her pulse scrambling. Slowly, wishing he wasn't so obviously aware of her reaction, she drew her hand away. "I'm going to fix breakfast."

"Is it all right if I have a shower?"

"Sure. I'll show you where everything is." More comfortable with something practical to do, she led the way down the hall. "Clean towels in the closet." She opened a narrow louvered door. "Here's a razor if you want to shave." She offered him a disposable safety razor and a can of shaving cream. "Something wrong?" He was staring at the items she offered as though they were instruments of torture. "I guess you're used to an electric," she said, "but I don't have one."

"No." He managed a weak smile, hoping he wouldn't slit his throat. "This is fine."

"Toothbrush." Trying not to stare at him, she handed him a spare that was still in its box. "We don't have an electric one of these, either."

"I'll, ah, rough it."

"Fine. Take whatever looks like it will fit out of the bedroom. There should be jeans and sweaters. I'll have something ready in a half hour. Time enough?"

"Sure."

Cal was still staring at the toiletries in his hands when she shut the door.

Fascinating. Now that he was over the panic, the fear and the disbelief, he was finding the whole episode fascinating. He studied the cardboard box and toothbrush with a grin, like a boy who'd found a fabulous puzzle under the Christmas tree.

They were supposed to use these things three times a day, he remembered. He'd read all about it. They had different flavors of paste that they scrubbed all over their teeth. Sounded revolting. Cal squirted a dab of the shaving cream on his finger. Gamely he touched it to his tongue. It was revolting. How had anyone tolerated it? Of course, that had all been in the days before tooth and gum diseases had been eradicated by fluoratyne.

After opening the box, he ran a thumb over the bristles. Interesting. He grimaced into the mirror, studying his strong white teeth. Maybe he shouldn't take any chances.

Setting everything on the sink, he turned to look at the bathroom. It was like something out of those old videos, he thought. The clunky oval tub, with its single awkward-looking shower head sticking out of the wall. He would start filing it all away. Who could tell, maybe he'd write a book when he got home.

Of more immediate importance was figuring out how to operate the shower. Above the lip of the tub were three round white knobs. One was marked *H,* another *C,* and the middle was graced with an arrow. Cal scowled at them. He could certainly figure out that they meant Hot and Cold, but it was a far cry from the individual temperature settings he was accustomed to. There would be no stepping inside and telling the computerized unit he wanted ninety-eight degrees at a mist. It was fend-for-yourself.

He scalded himself first, then froze, then scalded himself again before he and the shower began to understand each other. Once it was running smoothly he could appreciate the feel of hot water beating down on his skin. He found a bottle marked Shampoo, took a moment to be amused by the packaging, then dumped some in his hand.

It smelled like Libby.

Almost immediately his stomach muscles tightened, and a wave of desire flowed over him, as hot as the water on his back. That was odd. Baffled, he continued to stare down at the pool of shampoo. Attraction had always been easy—simple, basic. But this was painful.

He pressed a hand to his stomach and waited for it to pass. But it persisted.

It probably had to do with the accident. That was what he told himself, and what he preferred to believe. When he got back home he'd have to check into a rest center for a full workup. But he'd lost his pleasure in the shower. He toweled off quickly. The scent of soap and shampoo—and Libby—was everywhere.

The jeans were a little loose in the waist, but he liked them. Natural cotton was so outrageously expensive that no one but the very rich could afford it. The black roll-necked sweater had a hole in the cuff and made him feel at home. He'd always preferred casual, comfortable clothes. One of the reasons he'd left the ISF was that they had a penchant for uniforms and polish. Barefoot and pleased with himself, he followed the scents of cooking into the kitchen.

She looked great. Her baggy pants accentuated her slenderness and made a man imagine all the curves and angles beneath the material. He liked the way she'd pushed the sleeves of the bulky red sweater up past her elbows. She had very sensitive elbows, he recalled, and felt his stomach knot again.

He wasn't going to think of her that way. He'd promised himself.

"Hi."

This time she was expecting him, and she didn't jump. "Hi. Sit down. You can eat before I check your bandage. I hope you like French toast." She turned, holding a plate heaped with it. When their eyes met, her fingers curled tight around the edges. She recognized the sweater, but it didn't remind her of her father when it was tugged over Cal's long, limber torso. "You didn't shave."

"I forgot." He didn't want to admit he'd been afraid to try his skill at it. "It stopped raining."

"I know. The sun's supposed to come out this afternoon." She set the platter down, then tried not to react when he leaned over her to sniff at the food.

"Did you really make that?"

"Breakfast is my best meal." She sat down, breathing a little sigh of relief when he took the seat across from her.

"I could get used to this."

"Eating?"

He took his first bite and let his eyes close with a sigh of pure pleasure. "Eating like this."

She watched him plow through the first stack. "How did you eat before?"

"Packaged stuff, mostly." He'd seen ads for complete meals in packages in the newspaper. At least there was some hope for civilization.

"I live like that myself most of the time. When I come

here I get the urge to cook, stack wood, grow herbs. The kind of things we did when I was a kid." And though she'd come here for solitude, she'd discovered she enjoyed his company. He seemed safe this morning, despite her initial reaction to the way he looked in the black sweater and trim jeans. She could almost believe she'd imagined the tense and unexpected little scene by the fire the night before.

"What do you do when you're not crashing planes?"

"I fly." He'd already thought his answer through and had decided it was best to stick as close to the truth as possible.

"Then you *are* in the service."

"Not anymore." He picked up his coffee and smoothly changed the subject. "I don't know if I've really thanked you properly for everything you've done. I'd like to pay you back for all this, Libby. Do you need anything done around here?"

"I don't think you're up to manual labor at this point."

"If I stay in bed all day again I'll go crazy."

She took a good look at his face, trying not to be distracted by the shape of his mouth. It was impossible to forget how close she'd come to feeling it on hers. "Your color's good. No dizziness?"

"No."

"You can help me wash the dishes."

"Sure." He took his first good look at the kitchen.

Like the bath, it distracted and fascinated him. The west
wall was stone, with a little hearth cut into it. There was
a hammered copper urn on the ledge stuffed with tall
dried flowers and weeds. The wide window over the
sink opened onto a view of mountains and pine. The
sky was gray and clear of traffic. He identified the refrigerator and the stove, both a glossy white. The wide
planked-wood floor shone with a polished luster. It felt
cool and smooth under his bare feet.

"Looking for something?"

With a little shake of his head, he glanced back at
her. "Sorry?"

"The way you were staring out the window, it seemed
you were expecting to see something that wasn't there."

"Just, ah…taking in the view."

Satisfied, she gestured toward his plate. "Are you
finished?"

"Yeah. This is a great room."

"I've always liked it. Of course, it's a lot more convenient with the new range. You wouldn't believe the
old museum piece we used to cook on."

He couldn't keep from grinning. "I'm sure I
wouldn't."

"Why do I get the feeling there's a joke and it's two
inches above my head?"

"I couldn't say." After picking up his plate, he moved
to the sink and began to open cupboards.

"If you're looking for a dishwasher, you're out of luck." Libby stacked the rest of the breakfast dishes in the sink. "My parents would never bend their sixties values that far. No dishwasher, no microwave, no satellite dish." She plugged the sink, then reached in front of Caleb for the bottle of dish detergent. "You want to wash or dry?"

"I'll dry."

He watched, delighted, as she filled the sink with hot, soapy water and began to scrub. Even the smell was nice, he thought, resisting the urge to bend down and sniff at the lemony bubbles.

Libby rubbed an itch on her nose with her shoulder. "Come on, Hornblower, haven't you ever seen a woman wash dishes before?"

He decided to test her reaction. "No. Actually, I think I did in a movie once."

With a bubbling laugh, she handed him a plate. "Progress steals all these charming duties from us. In another hundred years we'll probably have robots that will stack the dishes inside themselves and sterilize them."

"More like a hundred and fifty. What do you want me to do with this?" He turned the plate in his hand.

"Dry it."

"How?"

She lifted a brow and nodded toward a neatly folded cloth. "You might try that."

"Right." He dried the plate and picked up another. "I was hoping to go take a look of what's left of my sh—my plane."

"I can almost guarantee the logging trail's washed out. The Land Rover might make it, but I'd really like to give it another day."

He bit down on his impatience. "You'll point me in the right direction?"

"No, but I'll take you."

"You've already done enough."

"Maybe, but I'm not handing you the key to my car, and you can hardly walk that distance on those roads." She took the corner of his cloth and dried her hands while he tried to formulate a reasonable excuse. "Why wouldn't you want me to see your plane, Hornblower? Even if you'd stolen it, I wouldn't know."

"I didn't steal it."

His tone was just abrupt enough, just annoyed enough, to make her believe him. "Well, then, I'll help you find the wreckage as soon as the trail's safe. For now, have a seat and let me look at that cut."

Automatically he lifted his fingers to the bandage. "It's all right."

"You're having pain. I can see it in your eyes."

He shifted his gaze to meet hers. There was sympathy there, a quiet, comforting sympathy that made him want to rest his cheek on her hair and tell her everything. "It comes and goes."

"Then I'll check it out, give you a couple of aspirin and see if we can make it go again. Come on, Cal." She took the cloth from him and led him to a chair. "Be a good boy."

He sat down, flicking her a glance of amused exasperation. "You sound like my mother."

She patted his cheek in reply before taking fresh bandages and antiseptic from a cupboard. "Just sit still." She uncovered the wound, frowning over it in a way that made him shift uncomfortably in his chair. "Sit still," she murmured. It was a nasty cut, jagged and deep. Bruises the color of storm clouds bloomed around it. "It looks better. At least there doesn't seem to be any infection. You'll have a scar."

Appalled, he lifted his fingers to the wound. "A scar?"

So he was vain, she thought, more than a little amused. "Don't worry, it'll look dashing. I'd be happier if you'd had a few stitches, but I think that's more than my Sears and Roebuck degree can handle."

"Your what?"

"Just a joke. This'll sting some."

He swore, loudly and richly, when she cleaned the

wound. Before she was half finished, he grabbed her wrist. "Sting? Some?"

"Toughen up, Hornblower. Think about something else."

He set his teeth and concentrated on her face. The burning pushed his breath out in a hiss. Her eyes reflected both determination and understanding as she went competently about cleaning, treating and bandaging the wound.

She really was beautiful, he realized as he studied her in the watery early sunlight. It wasn't cosmetics, and it was highly unlikely that there had been any restructuring. This was the face she'd been born with. Strong, sharp, and with a natural elegance that made him long to stroke her cheek again. Her skin had been soft, he remembered, baby-smooth. And color had rushed in and out of it as her emotions had shifted.

Perhaps, just perhaps, she was an ordinary woman of her time. But to him she was unique and almost unbearably desirable.

That was why she made him ache, Cal told himself as he felt the muscles in his stomach knot and stretch. That was why she made him want her more than he'd ever wanted anything before, more than it was possible for him to want now. She was real, he reminded himself. But it was he who was the illusion. A man who had never been born, yet one who felt as though he had never been more alive.

"Do you do this often?" he asked her.

She hated knowing she was causing him pain, and she answered absently, "Do what often?"

"Rescue men."

He watched her lips curve and could almost taste them. "You're my first."

"Good."

"There, that should do."

"Aren't you going to kiss it and make it better?" His mother had always done so, as he imagined mothers had done for all time. When she laughed, he felt his heart lurch in his chest.

"Since you were brave." She leaned down and brushed her lips just above the bandage.

"It still hurts." He took her hand before she could move away. "Why don't you try again?"

"I'll get the aspirin." Her hand flexed in his. She would have backed away when he rose, but something in his eyes told her it would do no good. "Caleb…"

"I make you nervous." His thumb caressed her knuckles. "It's very stimulating."

"I'm not trying to stimulate you."

"Apparently you don't have to try." She was nervous, he thought again, but not frightened. He would have stopped if he'd seen fear. Instead, he brought her hand to his lips, then turned the palm upward. "You have wonderful hands, Libby. Gentle hands." He saw the emotions flickering in her eyes—confusion, unease, desire. He concentrated on the desire and drew her closer.

"Stop." She was appalled by the lack of conviction in her own voice. "I told you, I…" He brushed his lips against her temple, and her knees turned to water. "I'm not going to bed with you."

With a quiet murmur of agreement, he ran his hand up her back until her body was fitted against his. It amazed him how much he'd wanted to hold her like this. Her head nestled perfectly against his shoulder, as if they had been made to dance together. He had a moment's regret that there wasn't music, something low and pulsing. The thought made him smile. None of the women in his life had ever wanted to have the stage set. Nor had he ever had the urge to set one before.

"Relax," he murmured, and slid his hand up to the back of her neck. "I'm not going to make love with you. I'm only going to kiss you."

Panic had her straining away. "No, I don't…"

The fingers at the back of her neck shifted, tightened, held firm. Later, when she could think, she would tell herself that he had inadvertently touched some nerve, some secret vulnerability. An unspeakable pleasure sprang into her, and her head fell back in submission.

On the heels of that flash of sensation he brought his lips to hers.

She went rigid, though not from fear, not from anger, and certainly not in resistance. It was shock, wave after wave of it. A live wire, she thought dimly. Somehow she had closed her hand over a live wire, and the voltage was deadly.

His lips barely touched hers, teasing, titillating, tormenting. It was a caress, mouth against mouth, unbearably erotic. Then it was a nibble, an almost playful nibble. And a caress again, sweet and light and compelling. His lips were warm and smooth as they rubbed a whispering trail over hers. In arousing contrast, the stubble of his beard scraped roughly over her cheek as he turned his head to trace the outline of her lips with his tongue.

It was intimate, impossibly so, the way he tasted her, toyed with her. His tongue dipped to hers, savoring dark new flavors, before he changed the mood again and caught her bottom lip between his teeth, nipping, stopping unerringly at a point between pleasure and pain.

It was seduction, the kind she had never dreamed of. Slow, soft-edged, inescapable seduction. She could hear the low, helpless sound that caught in her throat as he closed his teeth lightly over her chin.

The hand that had tensed against his chest began to tremble. She felt the solid cabin floor sway under her feet. Her rigidity melted degree by degree until she was shuddering with the heat and pliant in his arms.

He'd never experienced anything, anyone, like her. It was as though she had melted against him, quietly, completely. Her taste was fresh, like the air that wafted through the open window. He heard the soft, yielding sound of her sigh.

Then her arms were around him, clinging. She plunged her fingers deep into his hair as she strained against him. In a heartbeat, her mouth went from submissive to avid, pressing hungrily, possessively, desperately, against his. Rocked by the force, he dived into the kiss and let passion rule.

She wanted…too much. Why hadn't she known she'd been starving? Just the taste of him made her ravenous. Her body felt as though it would explode as dozens of new sensations arrowed into it, each of them sharp, separate and stunning. A muffled cry escaped her when his arms tightened painfully around her. She was no longer trembling—but he was.

What was she doing to him? He couldn't catch his breath. He couldn't think. But he could feel—too much, too quickly. The loss of control was more dangerous to a pilot than an uncharted meteor storm. He'd only meant to give and take a moment of pleasure, to satisfy a simple need. But this was more than pleasure, and it was far from simple. He needed to pull back before he was sucked into something he didn't yet understand.

He drew her away with unsteady hands. It helped—a little—that her breathing was as ragged as his. Her eyes were wide and stunned. Yes, stunned was the word, he decided. He felt as though he'd flown into the side of a building.

What had he done? Confused, she lifted a hand to her lips. What had she done? She could almost feel her blood bubbling through her veins. Libby took a step back, wanting to find solid ground again, and easy answers.

"Wait." He couldn't resist. He might curse himself for it later, but he couldn't resist. Before the first shock waves had passed, he hauled her against him a second time.

Not again. The single thought echoed in both their minds as they went under. The pull was just as strong, the need just as gripping. She felt herself seesaw between limp surrender and furious demand before she managed to yank herself free.

She nearly stumbled, and caught the back of a kitchen chair to steady herself. Her knuckles went white on the wood as she stared at him, dragging air into her lungs. She knew nothing about him, yet she had given him more than she had ever given anyone. Her mind was trained to ask questions, but at the moment it was her heart, fragile and irrational, that held sway.

"If you're going to stay here, in this house, I don't want you to touch me again."

It was fear he saw in her eyes now. He understood it, as he felt a trace of it himself. "I didn't expect that any more than you did. I'm not sure I like it any more than you do."

"Then we shouldn't have any trouble avoiding anything like this in the future."

He tucked his hands in his pockets and rocked back on his heels, not bothering to analyze why he was suddenly so angry. "Listen, babe, that was just as much your doing as mine."

"You grabbed me."

"No, I kissed you. You did the grabbing." It gave him little satisfaction to see her color rise. "I didn't force myself on you, Libby, and we both know it. But if you want to pretend you've got ice in your veins, that's fine with me."

The embarrassed flush fled from her face, leaving it very white and very still. In contrast, her eyes went dark and wide. The stunned hurt that glazed them had him cursing himself and stepping forward.

"I'm sorry."

She shifted behind the chair and managed to speak

calmly. "I don't want or expect an apology from you, but I do expect cooperation."

His eyes narrowed. "You'll get both."

"I have a lot of work to do. You're welcome to take the television into your room, and there are books on the shelf by the fireplace. I'd appreciate it if you'd stay out of my way for the rest of the day."

He dug his hands into his pockets. If she wanted to be stubborn, he could match her. "Fine."

She waited, her arms crossed over her chest, until he strode out of the room. She wanted to throw something, preferably something breakable. He had no right to say that to her after what he'd made her feel.

Ice in her veins? No, her problem had always been that she felt too much, wanted too much. Except when it came to personal, physical, one-to-one relationships with men. Miserable, she yanked out the chair and dropped onto it. She was a devoted daughter, a loving sister, a faithful friend. But no one's lover. She'd never experienced the driving need for intimacy. At times she'd been certain there was something lacking in her.

With one kiss, Cal had made her want things she'd almost convinced herself weren't important. At least not for her. She had her work, she was ambitious, and she knew she would make her mark. She had her family, her friends, her associates. Damn it, she was happy. She didn't need some hotshot pilot who couldn't keep his plane in the air to come along and make her feel restless—and alive, she mused, running a fingertip over her bottom lip. She hadn't known just how alive she could feel until he'd kissed her.

It was ridiculous. More unnerved than annoyed, she sprang up to pour another cup of coffee. He'd simply reminded her of something she forgot from time to time. She was a young, normal, healthy woman. A woman, she remembered, who had just spent several months on a remote island in the South Pacific. What she needed was to finish her dissertation and get back to Portland. Socialize, take in some movies, go to a few parties. What she needed, she decided with a nod, was to get Caleb Hornblower on his way, back to wherever the devil he came from.

Taking the coffee, she started upstairs. For all she knew, he might have dropped down from the moon.

She passed his room and couldn't prevent a quick snicker when she heard the frantic sounds of a television game show. The man, she thought as she slipped behind her own door, was easily entertained.

Chapter 4

It was an education. Cal spent several hours engrossed in a sea of daytime television. Every ten or fifteen minutes he switched channels, moving from game show to soap opera, from talk show to commercial. He found the commercials particularly entertaining, with their bright, often startling, intensity.

He preferred the musical ones, with their jumpy tunes and contagious cheer. But others made him wonder about the people who lived in this time, in this place.

Some selections showcased frazzled women fighting things like grease stains and dull wax buildup. He couldn't imagine his mother—or any other woman, for that matter—worrying about which detergent made whites whiter. But the commercials were delightful entertainment.

There were others that had attractive men and women solving their problems by drinking carbonated beverages or coffee. It seemed everyone worked, many outside, in sweaty jobs, so that they could go to a bar with friends at the end of the day and drink beer. He thought their costumes were wonderful.

On a daytime drama he watched a woman have a brief, intense conversation with a man about the possibility of her being pregnant. Either a woman was pregnant or she wasn't, Cal mused, switching over to see a paunchy man in a checked jacket win a week's vacation in Hawaii. From the winner's reaction, Cal figured that must be a pretty big deal in the twentieth century.

He wondered, as he caught snippets of *The News At Noon*, how humanity had ever made it to the twenty-first century and beyond. Murder was obviously a popular sport. As were discussions on arms limitations and treaties. Politicians apparently hadn't changed much, he thought as he snacked on a box of cookies he'd found in Libby's kitchen, his legs folded under him. They were still long-winded, they still danced around the truth, and they still smiled a great deal. But to imagine that world leaders had actually negotiated over how many nuclear weapons each would build and maintain was ludicrous. How many had they thought they needed?

No matter, he decided, and switched back to a soap. They had come to their senses eventually.

He liked the soaps the best. Though the picture was wavy and the sound occasionally jumped, he enjoyed watching the people react, agonizing about their problems, contemplating marriages, divorces and love affairs. Relationships had apparently been among the top ten problems of this century.

As he watched, a curvy blonde with tears in her eyes and a tough-looking bare-chested man fell into each other's arms for a long, deep, passionate kiss. The music swelled until fade-out. Kissing was obviously an accepted habit of the time, Cal reflected. So why had Libby been so upset by one?

Restless, he rose and walked to the window. He hadn't exactly reacted in an expected fashion himself. The kiss had left him feeling angry, uneasy and vulnerable. None of those reactions had ever occurred before. And none of them, he admitted now, had lessened his desire for her in the least.

He wanted to know everything there was to know about Liberty Stone. What she thought, what she felt, what she wanted most, what she liked the least. There were dozens of questions he wanted to ask her, dozens of ways he wanted to touch her, and he knew that when he did her eyes would become dark and confused and depthless. He could imagine, with only the slightest effort, what her skin would feel like on the back of her knee, at the small of her back.

It was impossible. There was only one thing he should be thinking about now. Going home.

The time with Libby was only an interlude. Knowing as little as he did about women of this time didn't prevent him from being certain that Liberty Stone was not a woman a man could love and leave with any comfort. One look in her eyes and you saw not only passion but home fires burning.

He was a man who had no intention of settling down anytime soon. True, his parents had matched early and had married fairly young, at thirty. But he had no desire to be matched, mated or married yet. And when he did, Cal reminded himself it would be on his own ground. He would think of Libby only as a distraction, however pleasant, in a tense and delicate situation.

He needed to be gone. He pressed his palms against the cool glass of the window as if it were a prison he could easily escape. This was an experience some men might have craved, but he preferred breaking the boundaries of his own world—and his own time.

True, he'd learned things by reading the newspapers and watching the television. In the twentieth century the world was a long way from reaching peace, people worried a great deal about what to have for dinner and weapons were owned and used with reckless abandon. A dozen farm-fresh eggs could be had for about a dollar—which was the current U.S. currency—and everyone was on a diet.

It was all very interesting, but he didn't think any of this information was going to help. He had to concentrate on taking his mind back to what had happened on board his ship.

But he wanted to think about Libby, about what it had felt like to hold her against him. He wanted to remember how she had heated, about the way her lips had softened when his had met them.

When her arms had come around him, he had trembled. That had never happened to him before. He had what he considered a normal, healthy track record with women. He enjoyed them, both for company and for mutual physical pleasure. Since he believed in giving as much as he took, most of his lovers had remained his friends. But none of them had ever made his system churn as it had during one kiss with Libby.

All at once she'd taken him beyond what he knew and into some wild, gut-wrenching spin. Even now he could remember what it had felt like when her lips had gone hot and urgent against his. His balance had tilted. He'd almost believed he saw lights whirling behind his eyes. It had been like being pulled toward something of enormous, limitless force.

His legs turned to water under him. Slowly he lifted

a hand to brace himself against the wall. The dizziness passed, leaving a hollow throbbing at the base of his skull. And suddenly he remembered. He remembered the lights. The flashing, blinking lights in the cockpit. Navigational system failed. Shields inoperative. Automatic distress signal engaged.

The void. He could see it, and even now the sweat pearled cold on his brow. A black hole, wide and dark and thirsty. It hadn't been on the charts. He would never have wandered so close if it had been on the charts. It had just been there, and his ship had been dragged toward it.

He hadn't gone in. The fact that he was alive and undoubtedly on Earth made him certain of that. It was possible that he had somehow skimmed the edge of it, then shot like a rubber band through space and time. The scientists of his era would question that idea. Time travel was only a theory, and one that was usually laughed at.

But he'd done it.

Shaken, he sat on the edge of the bed. He'd survived what no one in recorded history had survived. Lifting his hands, he turned the palms upward and stared at them. He was whole, and relatively undamaged. And he was lost. He fought back a fresh wave of panic, balling his hands into fists. No, not lost—he wouldn't accept that. If he had been shot one way, it was only logical that he could be shot another. Back home.

He had his mind, and his skill. He glanced at his wrist unit. He could work some basic computations on it. It wouldn't be enough, it wouldn't be nearly enough, but when he got back to his ship… If there was anything left of his ship.

Refusing to consider the fact that it might be completely destroyed, he began to pace. It was possible that he could interface his mini with Libby's machine. He had to try.

He could hear her downstairs. It sounded as though she were in the kitchen again, but he doubted she would fix him another meal. The regret came, too quickly to block, and the image of her sitting across the table from him flashed through his mind. He couldn't afford regrets, Cal reminded himself. And, if there was any choice, he wouldn't hurt her.

He'd apologize again, he decided. In fact, if he was successful with her computer, he would get out of her life as smoothly and painlessly as possible.

He moved quickly, quietly, into her room. He could only hope she would stay occupied until he made a few preliminary calculations. He'd have to be satisfied with those until he could find his ship and employ his own computer. Though impatience pushed at him, he hesitated for another moment, listening at the doorway.

She was definitely in the kitchen, and, judging by the banging going on, she was still in a temper.

The computer, with its awkward box screen and its quaint keyboard, sat on the desk, surrounded by books and papers. Cal sat in Libby's chair and grinned at it.

"Engage."

The screen remained blank.

"Computer, engage." Impatient with himself, Cal remembered the keyboard. He tapped in a command and waited. Nothing.

Sitting back, he drummed his fingers on the desk and considered. Libby, for reasons Cal couldn't fathom, had shut the machine down. That was easily remedied. He pushed through a few papers and picked up a letter opener. He turned the keyboard over, preparing to pry off the face. Then he saw the switch.

Idiot, he said to himself. They had switches for everything here. Calling on his remaining patience, he turned on the keyboard, then searched for more switches on the unit. When it began to hum, he had to muffle a cry of triumph.

"Now we're getting somewhere. Computer—" He caught himself with a shake of the head and began to type.

Computer, evaluate and conclude time warp factor—

He stopped himself again, swore, then pried off the plastic cover to reveal the memory board. His impatience was making him sloppy. And—worse—stupid. You couldn't get anything out of a machine that hadn't been put in. It was delicate, time-consuming work, but he forced himself not to rush. When he was finished, it was jury-rigged at best, but his wrist unit was interfaced with Libby's computer.

He took a deep breath and crossed the fingers on both hands. "Hello, computer."

Hello, Cal. The tinny words beeped from his wrist unit as the letters flashed across Libby's screen.

"Oh, baby, it's good to hear from you."

Affirmative.

"Computer, relay known data on theory of time travel through force of gravity and acceleration."

Untested theory, first proposed by Dr. Linward Bowers, 2110. Bowers hypothesized—

"No." Cal dragged a hand through his hair. In his hurry, he was getting ahead of himself. "I don't have time for all of that now. Evaluate and conclude. Time travel and survival probability on encounter with black hole."

Working... Insufficient data.

"Damn it, it happened. Analyze necessary acceleration and trajectory. Stop." He heard Libby coming up the stairs and had time only to shut down the unit before she stepped inside.

"What are you doing?"

Trying for a look of innocence, Cal smiled and swung out of the chair. "I was looking for you."

"If you've messed with my machine…"

"I couldn't help glancing at your papers. Fascinating stuff."

"I think so." She frowned at her desk. Everything seemed in order. "I could have sworn I heard you talking to someone."

"No one here but you and me." He smiled again. If he could distract her for a few minutes, he could disengage his unit and wait for a safer time. "I was probably mumbling to myself. Libby…" He took a step toward her, but she thrust a tray at him.

"I made you a sandwich."

He took the tray and set it on the bed. Her simple kindness left him feeling as guilty as sin. "You're a very nice woman."

"Just because you annoy me doesn't mean I'd starve you."

"I don't want to annoy you." He stepped over quickly when she wandered toward the computer. "I don't seem to be able to avoid it. I'm sorry you didn't like what happened before."

She cast him a quick, uneasy glance. "That's better forgotten."

"No, it's not." Needing the contact, he closed a hand over hers. "Whatever happens, it's something I won't forget. You touched something in me, Libby, something that hasn't been touched before."

She knew what he meant, exactly, precisely. And it frightened her. "I have to get back to work."

"Do all women find it difficult to be honest?"

"I'm not used to this," she blurted out. "I don't know how to deal with it. I'm not comfortable around men. I'm just not passionate."

When he laughed, she spun away, furious and embarrassed.

"That's the most ridiculous thing I've ever heard. You're overloaded with passion."

She felt something shift inside her, strain for freedom. "For my work," she said, spacing her words carefully. "For my family. But not in the way you mean."

She believed it, Cal decided as he studied her. Or she had made herself believe it. In the past two days he'd learned what it was like to doubt yourself. If he could repay her in no other way, perhaps he could show her what kind of woman she held trapped inside.

"Would you like to take a walk?"

She blinked at him. "What?"

"A walk."

"Why?"

He tried not to smile. She was a woman who would require reasons. "It's a nice day, and I'd like to see a little of where I am. You could show me."

She untangled the fingers she'd twisted together. Hadn't she promised herself she would take time to enjoy herself? He was right. It was a nice day, and her work could certainly wait.

"You'll need your shoes," she told him.

There was a scent to the cool, slightly moist air. Pine, he realized after several moments' mental debate. The scent was pine, like Christmas. But it came from the genuine article, not a scent disk or a simulator. The ground was thick with trees, and the breeze, though it was light, sounded through them like a sea. The clear pale-blue sky was marred only by the gray-edged clouds due north. There was birdsong.

But for the cabin behind them and a dilapidated shed, there were no man-made structures—just mountain, sky and forest.

"This is incredible."

"Yes, I know." She smiled, wishing it didn't please her quite so much that he appreciated and understood. "Whenever I come here, I'm tempted to stay."

He walked beside her, matching her pace, as they entered the sun-dappled forest. It didn't feel odd being alone with her now. It felt right. "Why don't you?"

"My work, primarily. The university wouldn't pay me to walk in the woods."

"What do they pay you for?"

"To research."

"When you don't research, how do you live?"

"How?" She tilted her head. "Quietly, I suppose. I have an apartment in Portland. I study, lecture, read."

The path was steeper now. "For entertainment?"

"Movies." She shrugged. "Music."

"Television?"

"Yes." She had to laugh. "Sometimes too often. What about you? Do you remember what you like to do?"

"Fly." His grin was quick and charming. She hardly noticed when he took her hand. "There's nothing else like it, not for me. I'd like to take you up and show you."

Her expression was bland as she glanced at the bandage on his head. "I'll pass."

"I'm a good pilot."

Amused, she reached down to pick a wildflower. "Possibly."

"Absolutely." In a move that was both smooth and natural, he took the flower from her and slipped it into her hair. "I had some trouble with my instruments, or I wouldn't be here."

Because the gesture threw her off, she stared at him for a moment before she began to walk again. "Where were you going?" She slowed her pace as Cal dallied, picking wildflowers along the trail.

"Los Angeles."

"You had a long way to go."

He opened his mouth, fooled for a moment into thinking she was making a joke. "Yes," he finally managed. "Longer than I anticipated."

Hesitantly she touched the blossom in her hair. "Will someone be looking for you?"

"Not for a while." He turned his face to the sky. "If we find my...plane tomorrow, I can assess the damage and go on from there."

"We should be able to drive into town in another day or two." She wanted to smooth away the worry line that had formed between his brows. "You can see a doctor, make some phone calls."

"Phone calls?"

His baffled look had her worrying about his head injury again. "To your family or friends, or your employer."

"Right." He took her hand again, absently sniffing at the clutch of flowers he held. "Can you give me the bearing and distance from here to where you found me?"

"Bearing and distance?" Laughing, she sat on the bank of a narrow, fast-running creek. "How about if I tell you it was that way?" She pointed toward the southeast. "Ten miles as the crow flies, double that by the road."

He dropped down beside her. Her scent was as fresh

as the wildflowers, and more alluring. "I thought you were a scientist."

"That doesn't mean I can give you longitude and latitude or whatever. Ask me about the mudmen of New Guinea and I'll be brilliant."

"Ten miles." Eyes narrowed, he scanned the fringe of fir. Where it thinned, he could see a towering, rough-edged mountain, blue in the sunlight. "And there's nothing between here and there? No city? No settlement?"

"No. This area is still remote. We get a few hikers now and again."

Then it was unlikely that anyone had come across his ship. That was one concern he could push to the back of his mind. His main problem now was how to locate his ship without Libby. The easiest way, he supposed, would be to leave at first light, in her vehicle.

But that was tomorrow. He was coming to understand that time was too precious, and too capricious, to waste.

"I like it here." It was true. He enjoyed sitting on the cool grass, listening to the water. It made him wonder what it would be like to come back to this same spot two centuries later. What would he find?

The mountain would be there, and possibly part of the forest that closed in around them. This same creek might still rush over these same stones. But there would be no Libby. The ache came again, dull and gnawing.

"When I'm home again," he said very slowly, "I'll think of you here."

Would he? She stared at the water, at the play of sunlight over it, and wished it didn't matter. "Maybe you'll come back sometime."

"Sometime." He toyed with her fingers. She would be a ghost to him then, a woman who had existed only in a flash of time, a woman who had made him wish for the impossible. "Will you miss me?"

"I don't know." But she didn't draw her hand away, because she realized she would miss him, more than was reasonable.

"I think you will." He forgot his ship, his questions, his future, and concentrated on her. He began to weave the flowers he'd picked through her hair. "They name stars and moons and galaxies for goddesses," he murmured. "Because they were strong and beautiful and mysterious. Man, mortal man, could never quite conquer them."

"Most cultures have some historical belief in mythology." She cleared her throat and began to pleat the baggy material of her slacks. "Ancient astronomers..." He turned her face to his with a fingertip.

"I wasn't talking about myths. Though you look like one with flowers in your hair." Gently he touched a petal near her cheek. "'There be none of Beauty's daughters/ With a magic like thee;/ And like music on the waters/ Is thy sweet voice to me.'"

It was a dangerous man, she knew instinctively, who could smile like the devil and quote poetry in a voice like silk. His eyes were the color of the sky just before dusk, a deep, dreamy blue. She'd never thought she was the kind of woman who could go weak just looking into a man's eyes. She didn't want to be.

"I should go back. I have a lot of work to do."

"You work too much." His brow rose when she turned her head aside and frowned. "What button did I push?"

Restless, more annoyed with herself than with him, she shrugged. "Someone always seems to be saying that to me. Sometimes I even say it to myself."

"It isn't a crime, is it?"

She laughed because his question seemed so sincere. "Not yet, anyway."

"It's not a crime to take a day off?"

"No, but—"

"No's enough. Why don't we say 'It's Miller Time'?" At her baffled look, he spread his hands. "You know, like on the commercials."

"Yes, I know." Hooking an arm around one upraised knee, she studied him. Poetry one moment, beer commercials the next. "Every now and again, Hornblower, I wonder if you're for real."

"Oh, I'm real." He stretched out to watch the sky. The grass was cool and soft beneath him, and the wind played lazily through the trees. "What do you see? Up there?"

She tilted her head back. "The sky. A blue one, thank goodness, with a few clouds that should clear by evening."

"Don't you ever wonder what's beyond it?"

"Beyond what?"

"The blue." With his eyes half-closed, he imagined... the endless sweep of stars, the pure black of space, the beautiful symmetry of orbiting moons and planets. "Don't you ever think about the worlds up there, just out of reach?"

"No." She saw only the arc of blue, speared through by mountains. "I suppose it's because I think more about worlds that were. My work usually keeps my feet, and my eyes, on the ground."

"If there's going to be a world tomorrow, you have to look to the stars." He caught himself. It seemed foolish to pine for something that might be lost. How odd it was that he was thinking so much of the future, and Libby so much of the past, when they had the here and now.

"What movies and music?" he asked abruptly. Libby shook her head. There seemed to be no order to his thought patterns. "Before, you said you liked movies and music for fun. Which ones?"

"All sorts. Good or bad. I'm easily entertained."

"Tell me your favorite movie."

"That's difficult." But his eyes were so intense, so earnest, that she picked one at random from her list of favorites. *"Casablanca."*

He liked the sound of it, the way she said it. "What's it about?"

"Come on, Hornblower, everyone knows what it's about."

"I missed it." He gave her a quick, guileless smile that no woman should have trusted. "I must have been busy when it came out."

She laughed again, with a quick shake of her head, a brightening of her eyes. "Sure. Both of us must have had pretty full schedules in the forties."

He let that pass. "What was the story?" He didn't care about the plot. He only wanted to hear her talk, to watch her as she did.

To humor him, and because it was easy to sit by the water and daydream, she began. He listened, enjoying the way she told the tale of lost love, heroism and sacrifice. Even more, he enjoyed the way she gestured with her hands, the way her voice ebbed and flowed with her feelings. And the way her eyes mirrored them, darkening, softening, when she spoke of lovers reunited, then pulled apart, by destiny.

"No happy ending," Cal murmured.

"No, but I always felt that Rick found her again, years later, after the war."

"Why?"

She had settled back, pillowing her head on her folded arms. "Because they belonged together. When people do, they find each other, no matter what." She was smiling when she turned her head, but the smile faded slowly when she saw the way he was looking at her. As if they were alone, she thought. Not just alone in the mountains, but totally, completely alone, as Adam and Eve had been.

She yearned. For the first time in her life, she yearned—body, mind and heart.

"Don't." He said the word quietly as she started to scramble to her feet. The lightest touch of his hand on her shoulder kept her still. "I wish you weren't afraid of me."

"I'm not." But she was breathless, as if she'd already been running.

"Of what, then?"

"Of nothing." His voice could be so gentle, she thought. So terrifyingly gentle.

"But you're tense." With his long, limber fingers, he began to rub at the tight muscles of her shoulders. He shifted, and his lips skimmed over her temple, as cool and stirring as the breeze. "Tell me what you're afraid of."

"Of this." She lifted her hands to push against his chest. "I don't know how to fight what I'm feeling."

"Why do you have to?" He skimmed a hand down the side of her body, astonished by the grinding need in his own.

"It's too soon." But she was no longer pushing him away. Her resolve was melting in a flood of hot, hammering need.

"Soon?" His laugh was strained as he buried his face against her throat. "It's already been centuries."

"Caleb, please." There was an urgency in her voice, a plea that was at once weak and unarguable. He knew as he felt her body vibrate beneath his that he could have her. Just as he knew as he looked down at the clouded confusion in her eyes that once he had she might not forgive him.

Need jerked inside him. It was a new and frustrating sensation. He rolled to one side and stood, and with his back to her he watched the water ripple.

"Do you drive all men crazy?"

She brought her knees up tight against her breasts. "No, of course not."

"Then I'm just lucky, I guess." He lifted his eyes to the sky. He wanted to be back there, spearing through space. Alone. Free. He heard the grass rustle as she stood and wondered if he would ever truly be free again. "I want you, Libby."

She didn't speak. She couldn't. No man had ever said those three simple words to her before. If thousands had, it wouldn't have mattered. No one would ever have spoken them in just that way.

Pushed to the brink by her silence, he whirled around. He wasn't her amiable, slightly odd patient now, but a furious, healthy and obviously dangerous man.

"Damn it, Libby, am I supposed to say nothing, to feel nothing? Are those the rules here? Well, the hell with it. I want you, and if I stay near you much longer, I'm going to have you."

"Have me?" She'd been certain her system was too weak and warm for anger. But it filled her with a flash that had her body straightening like an arrow. "What? Like a shiny car on a showroom floor? You can want anything you like, Cal, but when those wants concern me I've got some say in it."

She was magnificent...unbearably vivid, with fury in her eyes and flowers clinging to her hair. He would remember her like this, always. He knew it, and he knew the memory would be bittersweet, and yet his temper pushed him forward.

"You can have all the say you like." Taking both her arms, he pulled her against him. "But I'll have something before I go."

This time she struggled. It was pride, pride and anger, that had her jerking free. Then his arms came around her, twin vises that clamped her body unerringly to his. She would have sworn at him, but his mouth closed hard over hers.

It was nothing like the first time. Then he had seduced, persuaded, tempted. Now he possessed, not as if he had the right, but simply taking it. Her muffled protest went unheeded, her struggles ignored. Panic skidded up her spine, then slid down again, overwhelmed by pure desire.

She didn't want to be forced. She didn't want to be left without choice. That was her mind talking. It was right; it was reasonable. But her body leaped forward, leaving intellect far behind. She reveled in the strength, in the tension, even in the temper. She met power with power.

She came alive in his arms, making him forget who and why and where. When he could taste her, hot and potent on his lips, no other world, no other time, existed. For him it was as new, as exciting, as frightening as it was for her. Irresistible. The thought didn't come to him. No thought could. But she was as irresistible as the gravity that held their feet on the ground, as compelling as the need that sent their pulses racing.

He dragged her head back and plunged into the velvet moistness of her waiting mouth.

The world was spinning. With a moan, she ran her hands up his back, until she was clinging desperately to his shoulders. She wanted it to go on spinning, whirling madly, until she was dizzy and breathless and limp. She could hear the murmur of the water, the whisper of the breeze through the pines. There was a strong shaft of sunlight on her back. She knew that in reality her feet were still on solid ground. But the world was spinning.

And she was in love.

The sound that came from deep in her throat was one of surrender. To him. To herself.

He murmured her name. A searing ache arrowed through him as desire veered painfully toward a new, uncharted emotion. The hand that had been roaming through her hair clenched reflexively. He felt the petals of a flower crush. The scent, sweet and dying, rose on the air.

He jerked away, appalled. The flower was in his hand, fragile and mangled. His gaze was drawn to her lips, still warm and swollen from his. His muscles trembled. A wave of self-disgust rose up inside him. Never, never had he forced himself on a woman. The idea itself was abhorrent to him, the most shameful of sins. The reality was unforgivable—most unforgivable because she mattered as no one else ever had.

"Did I hurt you?" he managed.

Libby shook her head quickly, too quickly. Hurt? she thought. That was nothing. Devastated. With one kiss he had devastated her, showed her that her will could be crumbled and her heart lost.

He wouldn't apologize. Cal turned away until he was certain he was under control enough to speak rationally. But he would not apologize for wanting, or for taking. He would have nothing else of her when he left.

"I can't promise that won't happen again, but I'll do my best to see that it doesn't. You should go back inside now."

And that was all? Libby wondered. After he had stripped her emotions to the bone he could calmly tell her to go back inside? She opened her mouth to protest, and she nearly took a step toward him before she stopped herself.

He was right, of course. What had happened should never happen again. They were strangers, whatever her heart told her to the contrary. Without a word, she turned and left him alone by the creek.

Later, when the sun and shadows had shifted, he opened his hand to let the wounded flower fall into the water. He watched it drift away.

Chapter 5

She couldn't concentrate. Libby stared at her computer screen, trying to work up some interest in the words she'd already written. The Kolbari Islanders and their traditional moon dance no longer fascinated her. She'd been certain work was the answer—an immersion in it. No one had ever distracted her from her studies before. In college she'd completed a thesis while her roommates threw an open-door pizza party. That single-minded concentration had followed her into her professional life. She'd written papers in tents by lamplight, read notes on the back of a jogging mule and prepared lectures in the jungle. Once a project was begun, nothing broke the flow.

As she read a single paragraph through for the third time, all she could think of was Cal.

It was a pity she hadn't had a greater interest in chemistry, she thought, pulling off her glasses to rub at her eyes. If she had, perhaps she would understand more clearly her reaction to him. Surely there was a book somewhere that would give her the information so that she could analyze it. She didn't want to feel without being able to list logical reasons why. Daydreaming about love and romance was one thing. Experiencing it was something else altogether.

This wasn't like her.

With a long sigh, she pushed away from the desk and folded her legs under her. Her eyes still on the screen, she propped her elbows on her knees and braced her chin on her fisted hands. She wasn't in love, she told herself. It had been a knee-jerk reaction to the intensity of the moment. People didn't really fall in love that quickly. They could be attracted, of course, even strongly attracted. For love, though, other factors had to be mixed in.

Common ground and common interests, Libby decided. That made good, solid sense to her. How could she be in love with Cal when the only interest he had that she knew about was flying? And eating, she added with a reluctant smile.

An understanding of each other's feelings, goals,

temperaments. Surely that was vital to love. How could she be in love when she didn't understand Caleb Hornblower in the least? His feelings were a mystery to her, his goals had never been discussed, and his temperament seemed to change by the hour.

He was troubled. A frown brought her brows together when she thought of the look that she so often saw in his eyes. Sometimes he made her think of a man who had taken a wrong turn on the freeway and ended up in a strange, foreign land.

Troubled, yes, but he was also just plain trouble, she reminded herself, trying to keep her compassion from outweighing her common sense. His personality was too strong, his charm too smooth, his confidence too high. She didn't have room in her neatly ordered life for a man like Cal. He would, simply by existing, cause chaos.

She heard him come in the kitchen door, and her body braced automatically. Just as her pulse speeded up and her blood ran faster. Automatically.

Disgusted with herself, she scooted her chair back to her desk. She was going to work. In fact, she was going to work straight through to midnight, and she wasn't going to give Cal another thought. She caught herself gnawing on her thumbnail again.

"Damn it, who is Caleb Hornblower?"

The last thing she'd expected from her muttered

question was an answer. The tinny, disembodied voice had her jolting. She grabbed the edge of her desk to keep from spilling out of her chair, then stared, open-mouthed, at her computer screen.

Hornblower, Caleb, Captain ISF, retired.

"Oh, my God." With a hand to her throat, she shook her head. "Now just hold on," she whispered.

Holding.

It wasn't possible, Libby told herself as she pressed an unsteady hand to her mouth. She had to be hallucinating. That was it. Emotional stress, overwork and the lack of a good night's sleep were causing her to hallucinate. Closing her eyes, she took three deep breaths. But when she opened them again, the words were still on the screen.

"What the devil is going on here?"

Information requested and relayed. Is additional data required?

With an unsteady hand, she pushed aside some of the papers on her desk and uncovered Cal's watch. She would have sworn the voice she had heard had come from it. No, it just wasn't possible. Using a fingertip, she traced a thread-slim transparent wire that ran from his watch to the computer's drive.

"What kind of game is he playing?"

Five hundred twenty games are available on this unit. Which would you prefer?

"Libby?" Caleb stood just inside the doorway, thinking fast. There was no use berating himself for being careless. In fact, he wondered if subconsciously he'd wanted to put himself in a position where he would be forced to tell her the truth. But now, when she turned, he wasn't certain that would be good for either of them. She wasn't just frightened, she was furious.

"All right, Hornblower, I want you to tell me exactly what's going on here."

He tried an easy, cooperative smile. "Where?"

"Right here, damn it." She jabbed a finger at the machine.

"You'd know more about that than I would. It's your work."

"I want an explanation, and I want it now."

He crossed to her. A quick scan of the screen had a smile tugging at his mouth. So she'd wanted to know who he was. There was some comfort in knowing she was as confused by him as he was by her—and as interested.

"No, you don't."

He said it quietly, and he would have taken her hand if she hadn't batted his away.

"I not only want one, I insist on one. You...you..." On a sound of frustration, she took another breath. He wasn't going to make her stutter. "You come in here and plug your watch into my machine, and—"

"Interface," he said. "If you're going to work on a computer, you should know the language."

She snapped her teeth together. "Suppose you tell me how you can interface a watch with a PC."

"A what?"

She couldn't prevent the smirk. "Personal computer. You'd better brush up on the language yourself. Now—answers."

He put a hand on each of her shoulders. "You'd never believe me."

"You'd better make me believe. Is that watch some kind of miniature computer?"

"Yes." He started to reach for it, but she slapped a hand down on his wrist.

"Leave it. I've never heard of any miniature computer that answers voice commands, interfaces with a PC and claims to play over five hundred games."

"No." He looked down at her angry eyes. "You wouldn't have."

"Why don't you tell me how to get one, Hornblower? I'll buy my father one for Christmas."

Pure good humor tilted the corner of his mouth. "Actually, I don't think that model's going to be on the market for a little while yet. Can I interest you in something else?"

She kept her eyes level with his. "You can interest me in the truth."

Stalling seemed to be the best approach. He turned her hand over and linked his fingers with hers. "The whole truth, or the simple parts?"

"Are you a spy?"

The last thing she'd expected was laughter. After his first chuckle it rolled out of him, warm and delighted. He kissed her, once on each cheek, before she could stop him.

"You didn't answer my question." She wiggled out of his hold. "Are you an agent?"

"What makes you think so?"

"A wild guess," she said, throwing up her hands and spinning around the room. "You crash down in the middle of a storm no sensible person would have been driving in, much less flying. You have no ID. You claim you're not in the military, but you were wearing some kind of weird uniform. Your shoes were nearly falling apart, but you have a watch that makes a Rolex look like a Tinkertoy. A watch that talks back." Even as she said it, it seemed so preposterous that she looked at the screen to make certain she hadn't imagined it all. "Look, I know intelligence agencies have some pretty advanced equipment. It might not be James Bond, but—"

"Who's James Bond?" Cal asked.

Bond, James. Code name 007. Fictional charac-

ter created by twentieth-century writer Ian Fleming.
Novels include—

"Disengage," Cal ordered, dragging a frustrated hand through his hair. One look at Libby's face told him he was in deep. "Maybe you should sit down."

With a weak nod, she sat on the edge of the bed.

Though it was a bit late for precautions, Cal unhooked the wire and slipped it and his unit into his pocket. "You want an explanation."

She wasn't so sure anymore. Calling herself a coward, she gave a quick, jerky nod. "Yes."

"Okay, but you're not going to like it." He sat in her chair and crossed his ankles. "I was making a routine run from the Brigston colony."

"Excuse me?"

"The Brigston colony," Cal repeated. Then he took the plunge. "On Mars."

Libby closed her eyes and rubbed a hand over her face. "Give me a break, Hornblower."

"I told you you wouldn't like it."

"You want me to believe you're a Martian."

"Don't be ridiculous."

She dropped her hand into her lap. "I'm ridiculous? You sit there and try to feed me some story about coming from Mars and *I'm* ridiculous?" For lack of anything better to do, she tossed a pillow across the room, then rose and began to pace. "Look, it's not as though

I'm prying into your personal life, or even that I expect some kind of humble gratitude for dragging you in out of that storm, but I think some mutual respect is in order here. You're in my home, Hornblower, and I deserve the truth."

"Yes, I think you do. I'm trying to give it to you."

"Fine." Temper wasn't going to help, she thought. She dropped back on the bed and spread her arms. "So you're from Mars."

"No, I'm from Philadelphia."

"Ah." She let out a long, relieved breath. "Now we're getting somewhere. You were on your way to Los Angeles when you crashed your plane."

"My ship."

Her face remained calm and impassive. "That would be your spaceship."

"You'd call it that." He leaned forward. "I had to reroute because of a meteor shower. I was off course... farther, I realize, than I had first thought, because my instruments were unstable. I ran into a black hole, an uncharted one."

"A black hole." She no longer felt like laughing. His eyes were absolutely sincere. He believed it, she realized as she folded her hands tightly in her lap. His concussion was obviously much more serious than she had originally thought.

"That's a compressed star. Very dense, very powerful. Its gravity sucks up everything—stellar dust, gas, even light."

"Yes, I know what a black hole is." She had to keep him calm, Libby reasoned. She would humor him, express a friendly interest in his story, then get him back into bed. "So you were flying your spaceship, ran into a black hole and crashed."

"In simple terms. I'm not sure exactly what happened. That's why I hooked my wrist unit up to your computer. I need more information before I can calculate how to get back."

"To Mars?"

"No, damn it. To the twenty-third century."

The small, polite smile froze on her face. "I see."

"No, you don't." He rose to prowl the room. Patience, he told himself. He could hardly expect her to accept in a moment what he still had trouble believing himself. "There have been theories about time travel for centuries. It's generally accepted that if a ship could get up the needed speed and slingshot around the sun it could pass through time. It's only theory at this point, because no one's sure how to keep the ship from being sucked into the sun's gravity and frying. The same holds true for a black hole. If I'd been pulled in, the power and radiation would have ripped the ship apart. It had to be blind luck, but somehow I hit on the right trajectory—the precise speed, distance, angle. Instead of being pulled in, I bounced off." He flicked the curtain aside to look out at the darkening sky. "And landed here, over two and a half centuries back in the past."

Libby rose to lay a hesitant hand on his shoulder. "You should lie down."

He didn't look back at her, didn't need to. "You don't believe me."

She opened her mouth, but she couldn't bring herself to lie to him. "You believe it."

He turned then. There was sympathy in her eyes, the warm golden glow of it. "How would you explain it?" He reached in his pocket for his unit. "How would you explain this?"

"There's no need for explanations now. I'm sorry I pressured you, Caleb. You're tired."

"You have no explanation. For this—" he dropped the unit in his pocket again "—or for me."

"All right. My theory is that you're part of an intelligence operation, perhaps some elite section of the CIA. You were probably burned out—stress, tension, overwork. When you crashed, the shock and trauma of your head injury pushed you over the edge. You don't want to be a part of what you were, so you've chosen to give yourself a different time, a different history."

"So you think I'm crazy."

"No." The compassion was back, in her eyes, in her voice. She touched her hand to the side of his face in a comforting gesture. "I think you're confused and you need rest and attention."

He started to swear, but he caught himself. If he continued to insist, he would only frighten her. He'd already caused her a great deal of trouble that she didn't deserve.

"You're probably right. I'm still shaky from the crash. I should get some rest."

"That's a good idea." She waited until he reached the door. "Caleb, don't worry. It's going to be all right."

He turned back, thinking this would be the last time he saw her. Purple twilight filled the window at her back, and she seemed to be standing at the edge of a mist. Her eyes were dark and full of compassion. He remembered how rich and sweet the flavor of her lips was. Regret struck him like a fist.

"You are," he said quietly, "the most beautiful woman I've ever seen."

She stared, speechless, at the door he closed behind him.

He didn't sleep. As he lay in the dark he could only think of her. He switched on the television and watched the figures move like ghosts over the screen. They were, he realized, more real than he.

She hadn't believed him. There was little surprise in that. But she had tried to comfort him. He wondered if she knew how unique she was, in this age or any other. A woman who was strong enough to live on her own yet fragile enough to tremble in a man's arms. His arms.

He wanted her. In the pearly-gray light of early dawn he wanted her almost more than he could stand. Just to hold her would be enough. To lie beside her with her head settled on his shoulder. In silence. He could think of no other woman he would be content to spend hours of silence with. If he had a choice…

But he had no choice.

He was lying across the bed fully dressed. Now he rose. He had nothing to take with him, and nothing to leave behind. Moving quietly downstairs, he slipped out of the house.

The Land Rover was parked near the porch steps, where she had left it the night she'd brought him home. He crossed to it, casting a final glance at Libby's window. He hated to leave her stranded. Later he'd break into a radio frequency and broadcast her location. Someone would come for her.

She'd be mad. The idea made him smile a little as he climbed into the driver's seat. She would curse him, hate him. And she wouldn't forget him.

Cal took a moment to be charmed by the old-fashioned instruments and controls. The birds were singing as he tested the steering wheel and pumped the gas pedal curiously.

There was a lever between the seats marked with numbers running from one to four in an H pattern. Gears clanked when he shoved the lever forward. Confident he had the skill to operate such a simple vehicle, he turned knobs. When he got no response he jiggled the gearshift while depressing the floor pedals. Through trial and error, he found the clutch and shifted smoothly into first gear.

A beginning, he decided, and wondered where the hell the designer had put the ignition.

"You're going to have a hard time starting it without this." Libby stood on the porch, one hand in a fist on her hip, the other aloft, with the ignition key dangling from her fingers.

She was mad, all right, Cal thought. But he didn't feel like smiling. "I was just…thinking about taking a ride."

"Were you?" She tugged her hastily donned sweater farther over her hips before she walked down the steps. "It's your bad luck I didn't leave the keys in the car."

So it took a key. He should have known. "Did I wake you?"

She jabbed a fist hard at his shoulder. "You've got nerve, Hornblower. Feeding me all that garbage last night so I'd feel sorry for you, then trying to steal my car. What were you going to do, hot-wire it and leave me stranded? I'd have thought a hotshot pilot like you would be able to do it faster, and quieter."

"I was just borrowing it," he said, though he doubted the difference would matter to her. "I thought you'd be better off if I drove out to where I wrecked by myself."

She'd trusted him, she thought, calling herself ten kinds of a fool. She'd felt sorry for him. She'd wanted to help him. Betrayal and fury had her clenching her fist until the key bit into her palm. She'd help him, all right.

"Well, you can stop thinking. Move over."

"I'm sorry?"

"I said move over. You want to go to the wreck, I'll take you to the wreck."

"Libby—"

"Move over, Hornblower, or that hole in your head's going to have company."

"Fine." Giving up, he eased himself over the gearshift and dropped into the passenger seat. "Don't say I didn't warn you."

"To think I was feeling sorry for you."

He watched, intrigued, as she pushed the key into a slot and turned. The engine roared to life. The radio blared, the windshield wipers swished, and the heater blasted.

"You really are a case," she muttered, switching knobs.

Before he could comment, she popped the clutch, rammed down on the gas and sent them speeding onto the narrow dirt road.

"Libby." He cleared his throat, then pitched his voice above the noise of the engine. "I was doing what I thought was best for you. I didn't want to involve you any more than I already have."

"That's swell." She yanked the gearshift back and sent stones flying. "Just who do you work for, Hornblower?"

"I'm an independent."

"Oh, I see." Her mouth tightened into a grim line. "You sell to the highest bidder?"

The renewed anger in her tone puzzled him. "Sure. Doesn't everyone?"

"Some people don't put a price on their loyalty to their country."

Cal pressed his fingers to his eyes. He hadn't realized they were back to that. "Libby, I am not a spy. I don't work for the CAI—"

"CIA."

"Whatever. I'm a pilot. I run supplies, people, equipment. I deliver to spaceports, colonies, labs."

"So you're playing that tune again." She gritted her teeth as she sent the Land Rover over a sloping bank and across a stream. Water gushed up the sides. "What are you claiming to be this time—an intergalactic truck driver?"

He lifted his hands, then let them fall. "Close enough."

"I'm not buying it anymore, Cal. I don't think you're crazy. I don't think you're deluded. So cut it."

"Cut what?" When she only hissed at him, he decided to try again, once more, calmly. "Libby, everything I told you is true."

"Stop it." If she hadn't needed both hands on the wheel, she might have slapped him. "I wish I'd never seen you. You literally fall into my life and make me care about you, make me feel things I've never felt before, and all you do is lie."

He saw only one option. On impulse, he reached out and turned off the key. The Land Rover bumped to a stop. "Now listen to me." With his free hand, he grabbed her sweater and yanked her around. "Damn it." The oath came out as a murmur when he saw her face. "Don't cry. I can't stand it."

"I'm not crying." She wiped angry tears away with the backs of her hands. "Give me back the key."

"In a minute." He released her, holding his hand palm-out in a gesture of truce. "I wasn't lying when I said I was leaving this morning because I thought it was best for you."

She believed him. And she hated herself because he could so easily make her believe. "Will you tell me what kind of trouble you're in?"

"Yes." Because he couldn't resist, he trailed a fingertip across her damp cheek. "After we've found the—where I went down—I'll tell you anything you want to know."

"No more evasions or ridiculous stories?"

"I'll tell you everything." He lifted her hand, then pressed his palm to hers. "You have my word. Libby..." He linked his fingers with hers. "What do I make you feel?"

She drew her hand away to grip the wheel. "I don't know, and I don't want to think about it."

"I'd like you to know that I've never had the same feelings for another woman as I have for you. I wish things could be different."

He was already saying goodbye, she realized. A rippling ache spread in her chest. "Don't. Let's just concentrate on what needs to be done." While she stared straight ahead, he slipped the key back into the ignition. "You were right up there," she told him as she switched it on. "At the curve. The best I could say is that you were coming from that direction. I got the impression when I saw you crash that you went down along that ridge somewhere." With a frown, she lifted a hand to shield her eyes. "Strange...it looks like there's a break in that bank of trees up there."

Not strange, Cal thought, when you considered that a ship over seventy meters long and thirty across had come down in them. "Why don't we take a look?"

Libby turned off the road and started up the rocky slope. The part of her that was still annoyed hoped the jostling ride gave Cal the willies. But when she glanced at him, he was grinning.

"This is great!" he shouted. "I haven't done anything like this since I was a kid."

"Glad you're having fun." She turned her attention back to driving and didn't notice when Cal pushed a series of buttons on his watch. Excitement began to drum in him as he studied the directional beam on one of the dials.

"Twenty-five degrees north."

"What?"

"That way." He used his other hand to gesture with. "It's that way. Two point five kilometers."

"How do you know?"

He sent her a brilliant smile. "Trust me."

They climbed the ridge to where the line of pines thickened. The scattered dogwoods were budded but not yet ready to bloom. Libby shivered once in the cool air before she shut the engine off. "I can't drive through this. We'll have to walk."

"It's not far." He was already out and offering an impatient hand. "A few hundred meters."

She kept her hand at her side as she stared at his watch. It was sending out a low, regular beep. "Why is it doing that?"

"It's scanning. It only has a range of ten kilometers, but it's fairly accurate." Holding his wrist out, he moved in a slow circle. "Since I doubt there's anything metallic as big as my ship around here, I'd say we've found it."

"Don't start that again." Libby pushed her hands into her pockets and started to walk.

"You're supposed to be a scientist," Cal reminded her as he fell into step beside her.

"I am a scientist," she muttered, "which is why I know that men do not bounce off black holes and drop into the Klamath Mountains on the way back from Mars."

He slung a friendly arm around her shoulders. "You're looking behind you, Libby, not ahead. You've never seen anyone who lived two centuries ago, but you know they existed. Why is it so difficult to believe that they exist two centuries in the future?"

"I hope they will, but I don't expect to offer them coffee." He wasn't crazy, she decided, but he was clever. "You told me you'd tell me the truth—all of the truth—when we found your plane. I'm holding you to that." She tossed up her head, then froze. "Oh, my God."

Less than twenty feet ahead she saw a gap in the trees, the break she had spotted from beneath the ridge. Up close it looked as though a huge sickle had sliced through the forest, hewing down a swath of evergreen and undergrowth more than thirty feet wide.

"But there was no fire." She had to quicken her pace to keep up with Cal. "What could have done all this?"

"That." When they reached the break, Cal pointed. There, nestling on the rocky, needle-strewn ground, was his ship. Trees, some of them thirty feet high, lay like pickup sticks around it. "Don't go any closer until I check for radiation," Cal warned, but he needn't have bothered. Libby couldn't have moved if she'd wanted to.

Using his wrist unit, he checked the level and gave a quick nod. "It's well within normal limits. The time warp must have neutralized any excess." He slipped an arm around her shoulders again. "Come on inside. I'll show you my etchings."

Dazed, silent, she went with him. It was huge, as big as a house, and like no plane she had ever seen. A military secret, she told herself. That was why Cal had been so evasive. But surely one man couldn't fly something so large.

The front was its narrowest point, blunted, somewhat bullet-shaped, before it curved out into the body. There were no wings. That thought caused an uneasy lurch in her stomach. It's shape reminded her of a stingray that scuttled across the ocean floor.

An experiment, she told herself as she climbed over a fallen pine.

The body was a dull metallic color not glitzy enough to be called silver. There were scrapes and dents and dust all over it. Like an old, reliable family car, she thought giddily.

The damage had happened in the accident, she decided, but it worried her more than a little that several of the dents looked old. The Pentagon or NASA or whoever had built it would certainly have taken better care of something that had to be worth millions of taxpayer dollars.

"You came in this thing by yourself," Libby managed when he leaped down the slight slope to run his hand over the side of the ship.

"Sure." His fingers moved over the metal in an unmistakable caress. "She handles like a dream."

"Who does it belong to?"

"It's mine." There was both pleasure and excitement in his eyes when he held up a hand to help her down. "I told you I didn't steal it."

As a wave of relief passed over him, he spun her in a circle, then kissed her hard on the mouth. Finding the taste alluring, he kept her feet an inch off the ground and lingered over a second kiss.

"Caleb—" Breathless, dizzy, she pushed away from him.

"Kissing you's become a habit, Libby." He circled her waist with his hand. "I've always had a hard time breaking habits."

He was just trying to distract her, she thought. And he was doing an excellent job of it. "Pull yourself together," she ordered. "Now we've found this...thing.

You promised me an explanation. We both know very well that nothing like this is owned by a private citizen. Spill it, Hornblower."

"It is mine," he told her, still grinning. "Or it will be after ten more payments." He pressed a button to open the hatch. Libby's mouth dropped open as a door lifted up silently. "Come on, I'll show you the registration."

Unable to resist, she walked up the two steps and into the cabin. It was as large as her living room and was dominated by a control panel. There were hundreds of colored buttons and levers in front of two high-backed black seats shaped like scoops.

"Have a seat," he said.

Staying close to the open hatch, she rubbed her arms to ward off a sudden chill. "It's, ah…dark in here."

"Oh, yeah." Crossing to a panel, he touched a switch. Libby let out a muffled shriek as the front of the craft opened. "I must have hit the shields when I started down."

She could only stare. Before her were the forest, the distant mountains and the sky. Strong sunlight poured through. You could hardly call it a windshield when it spanned twenty feet.

"I don't understand." Because she needed to, she moved quickly to one of the chairs and sat. "I don't understand any of this."

"I felt the same way a couple of days ago." Cal opened

a compartment, scanned through some material, then took out a small, shiny card. "This is my pilot's license, Libby. After you read it, take a nice long breath. It might help."

His picture was in the corner. His grin was as attractive and disarming as it was in the flesh. The ID claimed that he was a United States citizen and licensed to pilot all A to F model ships. It listed his height as 185.4 cm, his weight as 70.3 kg. Hair black, eyes blue. And his birth date was…2222.

"Oh, my God," Libby whispered.

"You forgot to take that breath." He closed a hand over hers on the card. "Libby, I'm thirty. When I left L.A. two months ago it was February, 2252."

"That's crazy."

"Maybe, but it happened."

"This is a trick." She pushed the card back into his hand and sprang up. Her heart was racing so hard and fast that she could feel it vibrating between her temples. "I don't know why you're doing this, but it's all some kind of elaborate trick. I'm going home."

She rushed toward the hatch just as the door closed. "Sit down, Libby. Please." He saw the wild, trapped look in her eyes and forced himself not to step toward her. "I'm not going to hurt you. You know that. Just sit down, and listen."

Because she was angry that she had tried to run, she walked stiffly back and sat down. "So?"

He sat opposite her, steepled his fingers and thought it all through. There were times, he supposed, when it was best to treat an abnormal situation as if it were normal. "You didn't have any breakfast," he said abruptly. Pleased with the inspiration, he opened a small door and took out a glossy silver pouch. "How about ham and eggs?" Without waiting for an answer, he swiveled, opened another door and tossed the pouch inside. He pushed a button, then sat smiling at her until a buzzer sounded. Taking a plate out of another compartment, he opened the door and scooped out a heap of steaming eggs loaded with chunks of ham.

Libby locked her icy hands in her lap. "You're full of tricks."

"No trick. Irradiation. Come on, taste." He held the plate under her nose. "They're not as good as yours, but they'll do in a pinch. Libby, you have to believe what's in front of your eyes."

"No." Very slowly, she shook her head from side to side. "I don't think I do."

"Not hungry?"

She shook her head again, more firmly this time. With a shrug, Cal plucked a fork from a drawer and dug in.

"I know how you feel."

"No, you don't." She took his advice, belatedly, and sucked in three long breaths. "You're not sitting in what looks like a spaceship having a conversation with a man who claims to be from the twenty-third century."

"No, but I'm sitting in my ship talking to a woman who's a couple of centuries older than I am."

She blinked at that, then found laughter—only slightly hysterical—bubbling out. "This is ludicrous."

"Oh, yeah."

"I'm not saying I believe it."

"Give it time."

Her hand was no longer cold, but it was still unsteady when she pressed it to her head. "I need to think."

"Fine."

With a sigh, she sat back and studied him. "I'll take that breakfast now."

Chapter 6

The eggs were bland, but they were certainly hot. Irradiated, Libby thought as she took a second bite. She'd heard of the controversial process for preserving food. Still, it was a far cry from a microwave TV dinner.

Somehow she'd woken up in the middle of a science-fiction movie.

"I keep telling myself there has to be another explanation."

Cal polished off his eggs. "Let me know if you find one."

Dissatisfied, she set her plate aside. "If all this is real, you seem to be taking it very calmly."

"I've had some time to get used to it. Are you going to eat the rest of that?"

She shook her head, then turned to stare through the clear shield. She saw a pair of elk meander into the trees about a hundred yards away. A beautiful sight, she mused. Beautiful, and normal here in the mountains of Oregon. If the elk had wandered down Fifth Avenue in Manhattan they would still have been beautiful, and they would still have been real. But, for reasons of basic geography, they wouldn't have been normal.

There was no denying that Cal was real. Was it possible that he and his incredible vehicle were a perfectly normal sight in another place? In another time?

If it were true...if she allowed herself for just one moment to believe it... How must he feel? She looked at the elk again. They were standing in a patch of sunlight. Mustn't he be feeling as confused and displaced as any animal taken out of its natural habitat and tossed into a strange world?

She remembered the panic she had seen on his face the day he'd come to her with a paperback novel. A novel published this year, Libby reflected. She'd dismissed his pallor, his dazed confusion, as the effects of his head injury. She'd discounted his odd questions and remarks the same way.

Now there was the ship—and no matter how far she stretched it she couldn't call the vehicle a plane. If she accepted that it was real and not part of some strange, vivid dream, then she had to accept Cal's story.

"'There are more things in heaven and earth, Horatio,/Than are dreamt of in your philosophy.'"

"Hamlet." He grinned at her quick, suspicious look. "We still read Shakespeare. Want some coffee?"

She shook her head. Dream or not, she needed answers. "You say you...bounced off a black hole?"

He smiled, immeasurably relieved. She believed him. Perhaps she didn't fully realize it herself, but she believed him. "That's right, or at least that's what I think. I'm going to need my computer. My instruments went berserk when we hit the gravitational field, so I went to manual and managed to bank east. I remember the force. It must be what a fly feels like when someone gives it a good solid bat. I passed out. When I came to, I was free-falling toward Earth. I switched back to computer and thought my troubles were over."

"That doesn't explain how you ended up here—or should I say now."

"There are a lot of theories. The one I lean toward deals with the space-time continuum. It's like a curved bowl." He cupped his palm to demonstrate. "Mathematically, the bowl isn't space and it isn't time. It's a combination of both. Everything in it moves through space and time. Gravity's the curve of the bowl, drawing everything down. Around the Earth it's not much of a curve. You don't really feel it unless you, say, fall off

a cliff. But around the sun, and around a black hole…"
He deepened the cup of his palm.

"And you're saying you were caught in that curve?"

"Like a marble being spun around the lip of the bowl.
And somewhere, somehow, along the spin, I was flicked
off. The speed, the trajectory, sent me tunneling not just
through space but through time."

"It sounds almost plausible when you say it."

"It's the only theory I've got. Maybe if we look at it,
it'll sound more plausible." Leaning forward, he turned
a dial. "Computer."

Yes, Cal.

Libby lifted a brow at the soft, sultry voice. "Since
when do they make computers tall, blond and busty?"

He just grinned. "Intergalactic runs can be lonely.
Computer, play back log date 02-05. On screen."

Cal swiveled in his chair and leaned forward as a
small viewing screen rose out of the console. Sound
filled the cockpit. Impassive, he watched his own image
flicker on. From her chair, Libby stared mesmerized, as
the playback progressed. She could see him sitting precisely where he was sitting now. But there were lights
flashing, buzzers sounding. While the cockpit vibrated,
he reached up to secure a safety strap. She could see
the sweat beading on his face as he fought the controls
of the bucking ship.

"Widen image," Cal commanded.

Then Libby saw what he had seen through the shield. There was the vastness of space, seductive and compelling. There were stars, clusters of them, and what was surely a distant planet. There was a blackness, an absolute blackness, that spread for miles. The ship seemed to be hurtling toward it.

She heard Cal swearing—or rather the image of Cal was swearing as he pulled on a lever. There was a sound, a screaming rip of metal that seemed to vibrate all around her. The cockpit began to roll, end over end, with sickening speed. And then the screen went blank.

"Damn it. Computer, continue playback."

Memory banks damaged. No further playback possible.

"Terrific." He started to command an analysis, but then he caught a glimpse of Libby. She was sitting limply in the chair beside his, her cheeks a dead white, her eyes glassy. "Hey." He was up quickly and leaning over her. "Take it easy." Cupping her face in his hands, he pressed his thumbs lightly on either side of her throat.

"It was like I was there."

He cursed himself and took her icy hand in his to warm it. He had known better, Cal thought in disgust. But he had only been thinking of himself and his need to see what had happened. "I know. I'm sorry."

"It was horrible." Whatever doubts she had harbored

had vanished completely during the playback. Her fingers tightened convulsively on his as she looked up at him. "It's all been horrible for you."

"No." He combed his fingers through her hair. "Not all." Softly, gently, he touched his lips to hers, then skimmed them over her jaw. She reached a hand to his face, letting it linger while she gave and took the comfort.

"What are you going to do?"

"I'm going to find a way back."

She felt a pain, sharp and sudden. Of course he couldn't stay. Carefully she laid her hand back in her lap. "When will you go?"

"It's going to take a little time." He straightened and glanced around the cabin. "I need to do some repairs on the body of the ship. There are a lot of calculations that have to be done."

"I'd like to help you." She made a helpless gesture with her hands. "I don't know how."

"I'd like you to stay while I'm working. I know you've got a lot to do, but if you could spare a few hours?"

"Sure." She dug up a smile. "I don't get many offers to spend the day in a spaceship." But she couldn't sit beside him at that moment. If he looked at her too closely he might see what she had just discovered: when he left he would break her heart. "Can I look around?"

"All you want." She was still pale, he noted, but her voice was strong. Perhaps, like him, she needed some time alone. "I'd like to get the computer started on some calculations."

She left him to it, trying not to jolt when automatic doors whispered open at her approach. She entered what seemed to be a small lounge. A pair of couches were built into the walls, curving back, then out, with bright orange cushions. A table of what appeared to be Lucite was bolted to the floor. There were a few glossy informational sheets tossed around. The future's version of *Car and Driver,* she thought with a nervous laugh as she chose one. She tapped it absently against her thigh as she wandered around the room.

She was a sensible woman, Libby told herself. A sensible woman accepted what couldn't be denied. But—

There were no buts. She was a scientist. One who studied man. For the time being, she would study what man would be rather than what he had been.

For an hour she walked through the ship, observing, absorbing. There was a narrow, untidy room she took to be the galley. There was no stove, only a wall unit that resembled a microwave. A refrigerator of sorts held a few bottles. The labels were a familiar red, white and blue and carried the name of a popular brand of American beer.

Man hadn't changed that much, Libby decided.

She chose an equally familiar brand of soft drink and twisted off the cap. She took a first experimental sip. Amazing, she thought as she took another. She might have found the bottle in her own refrigerator. Taking the bottle and its comforting familiarity with her, she wandered on.

She found herself in an enormous bay area. It was empty except for a huddle of boxes strapped into a corner.

He'd said he'd just made a supply run, she remembered. To Mars. When her stomach fluttered, she took another sip from the bottle.

So man had conquered Mars. Even in the twentieth century, scientists had been making plans to do so. She would have to ask Cal when the first colony had been built and how the colonists had been chosen. Slowly she rubbed her fingers against her temple. Perhaps in a day or two this would all seem less fantastic. Then she would begin to think logically and ask appropriate questions.

She continued through the ship. There was a second level that seemed to be comprised almost completely of bedrooms. Cabins, Libby corrected automatically. On ships they were called cabins.

The furniture was streamlined, and most of it was built directly into the wall. Smooth formed plastic and bright colors were the style.

She found Cal's almost by accident. She didn't want to admit she'd been looking. There was little difference between his and the other cabins, other than its homey untidiness. She saw a jumpsuit, similar to the one he'd been wearing when she'd found him, tossed in a corner. The bed was unmade. On the wall was a picture, eerily three-dimensional, of Cal standing with a group of people.

The dwelling behind them was multileveled and almost entirely glass. There were white terraces jutting out at all angles, and there were tall, shady trees on a green lawn.

This was his home, she thought, certain of it. And his family. She studied them again. The woman was tall and striking and appeared much too young to be his mother. A sister? she wondered, but then she remembered that he had spoken of only one brother.

They were all laughing. Cal had his arm slung around the shoulder of another man. The height and build were similar, and there was enough facial resemblance to make her certain that this was Cal's brother. His eyes were green, and even in the photograph they were uneasily piercing. A tough customer, she decided and shifted her attention to the third man in the photo.

He seemed slightly befuddled. His face wasn't as blatantly handsome, but there was kindness in it.

Trapped in time, she mused. That was what a photograph did. It trapped people in time. Just as Cal was trapped now. She lifted a hand, but she caught herself just before she stroked the image of his face.

It was important to remember that he was only here until he could break free. He had another life, in another world. What she was feeling about him, for him, was impossible. Just as impossible, she thought as she pressed the cool bottle to her brow, as the fact that she was standing in a vehicle designed to travel through space.

Abruptly weary, she sat down on the bed. It was crazy, all of it. And the craziest part of all was that she had fallen in love for the first time in her life. And the man she loved would soon be far beyond her reach. With a sigh, she stretched out on the slick, cool sheets. Perhaps it was all a dream after all.

He found her there more than an hour later, curled up on his bed. She was sleeping, as she had been the first time he remembered seeing her. It brought him an odd, unsettling feeling to watch her now.

She was lovely, but it was no longer her beauty that drew him. There was a sweetness about her, a combination of compassion and shyness. She had strength and passion. And innocence—an incredibly alluring innocence. He wanted to go to her now, to gather her up and make love with her in the softest, gentlest way he knew.

But she wasn't for him. He wished it could be like a fairy tale, wished she could go on sleeping for a hundred years, for two hundred and more, until he awakened her and claimed her for his own.

He wasn't a prince, he reminded himself. He was just an ordinary man caught in an extraordinary situation.

Moving quietly, he crossed to the bed to draw the sheet over her. She stirred, murmured. Unable to resist, he reached down to stroke her cheek. Her eyes fluttered open.

"Cal. I had the strangest dream." Then she was awake and pushing herself up to stare around the cabin. "Not a dream."

"No." He sat beside her. No matter how much he lectured himself, he couldn't deny the pleasure it gave him to share his bed with her, if only as a friend. "How do you feel?"

"Still a little rattled." She combed both hands through her hair, holding it away from her face for a moment before she let it fall. "I'm sorry, I didn't realize I'd fallen asleep. I guess my mind needed to shut off for a while."

"It's a little much to take in all at once. Libby?"

"Yes?" She glanced distractedly around the cabin, trying to let it all settle in.

"I'm sorry. I have to." He closed his lips over hers and savored. She was warm and soft from sleep. He couldn't have explained to her how badly he needed that yielding texture. Reflexively she lifted a hand to his shoulder. But there it relaxed.

It took all his willpower not to touch her and, with the need raw in his gut, to draw away.

"I lied," he murmured as his gaze dipped down to her mouth. "I'm not sorry." But he rose and moved away from the bed. She stood up and tried to keep her nervous fingers from fiddling with the hem of her sweater.

"Is that your family?"

"Yeah." He'd been staring at the picture, wishing life could be as simple as it had been at that moment. "My brother Jacob and my parents."

The love, somewhat wistful in his voice, was unmistakable. Moved by it, she laid a hand on his arm. "This is Jacob?" she asked, indicating his brother. "But they don't look old enough to be your parents."

"It isn't difficult to look young." He shrugged. "Well, it won't be."

"And that's your home?"

"I grew up there. It's about twenty kilometers outside the city limits."

"You'll get back to them." She buried her own yearnings. Love, no matter how suddenly it came or how deep it reached, was selfless. "Think of the story you'll have to tell."

"If I remember."

"But you couldn't forget." The possibility struck her

painfully. She couldn't bear it if he forgot her, if even her memory no longer existed. "I'll write it down for you."

He shook off his black mood and turned to her. "I'd appreciate that. Will you let me go back with you?"

She felt a flutter of hope. "Go back?"

"To the cabin. I've done about all I can for now. I can start the repairs on the ship tomorrow. I was hoping you'd let me stay until it's all ready."

"Of course." It was foolish, and selfish, to hope that he would stay any longer than necessary. She put on a bright smile as they started from the room. "I have dozens of questions to ask you. I don't even know where to begin."

Still, she asked him nothing on the drive back. He seemed distracted, moody, and her own mind was crowded with impressions and contradictions. It would be best, she decided, if they pretended a kind of normality for a few hours. Then, with a thud, inspiration hit.

"How would you like to have lunch in town?"

"What?"

"Try to stay tuned, Hornblower. Would you like to drive into town? You haven't seen anything but this little slice. If I suddenly found myself back in, say, the 1700s, I'd want to explore a little, watch people. It only takes a couple of hours. What do you say?"

The moodiness left his eyes, and he smiled. "Can I drive?"

"Not on your life." She laughed and tossed her hair back. "We'll stop back at the cabin for my purse."

It took more than thirty minutes to get to the highway through a narrow pass where the Land Rover had powered its way through the mud. When they reached the highway Cal saw the vehicles that had fascinated him on television. They rumbled noisily along. He shook his head as Libby jockeyed aggressively for position.

"I could teach you to fly a jet buggy in an hour."

The wind felt wonderful on her face. They had today, and perhaps a day or two more. She wasn't going to lose a moment of it.

"Is that a compliment?"

"Yeah. You're still using what—gasoline?"

"That's right."

"Amazing."

"Being smug and superior suits you—especially since you didn't even know how to turn my car on."

"I'd've figured it out." He reached out to touch the flying strands of her hair. "If I were home I'd fly you to Paris for lunch. Have you ever been there?"

"No." She tried not to think too deeply about the romance of it. "We'll have to settle for pizza in Oregon."

"Sounds great to me. You know, the strangest thing is

the sky. There's nothing in it." A car whizzed by, muf-
fler coughing, radio blaring. "What was that?"

"A car."

"That's debatable, but I meant what was the noise?"

"Music. Hard rock." She reached over to turn on the
radio. "That's not as hard, but it's still rock."

"It's good." With the music playing in his head, he
watched the buildings they passed. Neat single-family
homes, chunky apartment complexes and a spreading
single-level shopping center. The traffic thickened as
they came closer to the city. He could see the high
rectangular forms of office buildings and condos. It
was a cluttered and, to his eyes, awkward skyline, but
it was oddly compelling. Here were people, here life
continued.

Libby eased down the curving ramp and headed
downtown. "There's a nice Italian place, very traditional. Red checked tablecloths, candles in bottles,
hand-tossed pizza."

Cal gave an absent nod. There were people walking the sidewalk, some old, some young, some plain,
some pretty. There was noise from car engines, and the
occasional bad-tempered blare of a horn. The air was
warmer here and smelled slightly of exhaust. For him
it was a picture out of an old book come to life.

Libby pulled into a graveled lot next to a squat white-

and-green building. The neon sign across the front window said Rocky's.

"Well, it's not Paris."

"It's fine," he murmured, but he continued to twist his head and stare.

"It must feel like stepping through the looking glass."

"Hmm. Oh." He remembered the book, one he'd read as a teenager. "Something like that. More like something from H. G. Wells."

"It's nice to know literature has survived. Are you hungry?"

"I was born hungry." Once again he fought off a darkening mood. She was trying, and so could he.

The restaurant was dim, nearly empty, and the air simmered with spices. In the corner was a jukebox pumping out a current Top 40 hit. After a glance at a sign that read Please Seat Yourself, Libby led Cal to a corner booth. "The pizza's really wonderful here. Have you had pizza before?"

He flicked a finger at the hardened candle wax on the bottle in the center of the table. "Some things transcend time. Pizza's one of them."

The waitress toddled over, a plump young woman in a bright red bib apron that had Rocky's and a few splashes of tomato sauce dashed across the front. She placed two paper napkins beside place mats decorated with maps of Italy.

"One large," Libby said, taking Cal's appetite into account. "Extra cheese and pepperoni. Would you like a beer?"

"Yeah." He tore a corner from the napkin and rolled it thoughtfully between his thumb and forefinger.

"One beer and one diet cola."

"Why is everyone here on a diet?" Cal asked before the waitress was out of earshot. "Most of the ads deal with losing weight, quenching thirst and getting clean."

Libby ignored the quick curious look the waitress shot over her shoulder. "Sociologically our culture is obsessed with health, nutrition and physique. We count calories, pump iron and eat a lot of yogurt. And pizza," she added with a grin. "Advertising reflects current trends."

"I like your physique."

Libby cleared her throat. "Thanks."

"And your face," he added, smiling. "And the way your voice sounds when you're embarrassed."

She let out a long, windy sigh. "Why don't you listen to the music?"

"The music stopped."

"We can put more on."

"On what?"

"The jukebox." Enjoying herself, Libby rose and extended a hand to him. "Come on, you can pick a song."

Cal stood over the colorful machine, scanning the

titles. "This one," he decided. "And this one. And this one. How does it work?"

"First you need some change."

"I've had enough change for a while, thanks."

"No, I mean change. Quarters." Chuckling, she dug into her purse. "Don't they use coins in the twenty-third century?"

"No." He plucked the quarter from her palm and examined it. "But I've heard of them."

"We use them around here, often with reckless abandon." Taking the quarter back, she dropped it and two more into the slot. "An eclectic selection, Hornblower." The music drifted out, slow and romantic.

"Which is this?"

"'The Rose.' It's a ballad—a standard, I suppose, even today."

"Do you like to dance?"

"Yes. I don't often, but…" Her words trailed away as he gathered her close. "Cal—"

"Shh." He rubbed his cheek against her hair. "I want to hear the words."

They danced—swayed, really—as the music drifted through the speakers. A mother with two squabbling children rested her elbow on her table and watched them with pleasure and envy. In the glassed-in kitchen a man with a bushy mustache tossed pizza dough in quick, high twirls.

"It's sad."

"No." She could dream like this, with her head cushioned on his shoulder and her body moving to their inner rhythm. "It's about how love survives."

The words floated away. Her eyes were shut, her arms still around him when the next selection blasted out with a primeval scream and a thundering drum roll.

"What about this one?"

"It's about being young." She drew away, embarrassed, when she saw the smiles and stares of the other patrons. "We should sit down."

"I want to dance with you again."

"Some other time. People don't usually dance in pizza parlors."

"Okay." Obligingly he walked back across the room to their table. Their drinks were waiting. As Libby had with the drink in his galley, Cal found enormous comfort in the familiar taste of American beer. "Just like home."

"I'm sorry I didn't believe you at first."

"Babe, *I* didn't believe me at first." In a natural gesture he reached across the table to take her hand. "Tell me, what do people do here on a date?"

"Well, they…" His thumb was skimming over her knuckles in a way that made her pulse unsteady. "They go to movies or restaurants."

"I want to kiss you again."

Her eyes darted up to his. "I don't really think—"

"Don't you want me to kiss you?"

"If she doesn't," the waitress said as she plopped their pizza in front of them, "I get off at five."

Grinning, Cal slipped a slice of pizza onto a paper plate. "She's very friendly," he commented to Libby, "but I like you better."

"Terrific." She took a bite. "Are you always obnoxious?"

"Mostly. But I do like you, a lot." He waited a beat. "Now you're supposed to say you like me, too."

Libby took another bite and chewed it thoroughly. "I'm thinking about it." Taking her napkin, she dabbed at her mouth. "I like you better than anyone I've met from the twenty-third century."

"Good. Are you going to take me to the movies?"

"I suppose I could."

"Like a date." He took her hand again.

"No." Carefully she removed it. "Like an experiment. We'll consider it part of your education."

His smile spread, slow, easy and undoubtedly dangerous. "I'm still going to kiss you good-night."

It was dark when they returned to the cabin. More than a little frazzled, Libby pushed open the door and tossed her purse aside.

"I did not make a scene," Cal insisted.

"I don't know what they call being asked to leave a theater where you come from, but around here we call it making a scene."

"I simply made some small, practical comments about the film. Haven't you heard about freedom of speech?"

"Hornblower—" Stopping herself she held up a hand and turned to the cupboard to get the brandy. "Talking throughout the picture about it being a crock of space waste is not exercising the Bill of Rights. It's being rude."

With a shrug, he plopped down on the couch and propped his feet on the coffee table. "Come on, Libby, all that bull about creatures from Galactica invading Earth. I have a cousin on Galactica, and he doesn't have a face full of suction cups."

"I should have known better than to take you to a science-fiction movie." She sipped the brandy. Then, because she decided it was as much her fault as his, she poured another snifter. "It was fiction, Hornblower. Fantasy."

"Rot."

"All right." She passed him the snifter. "But there were people in the theater who had paid to watch it."

"How about that nonsense with the creatures sucking all the water out of the human body? Then there was the way that space jockey zipped around the galaxy shooting lasers. Do you have any idea how crowded that sector is?"

"No, I don't." She sampled more brandy. "Tell you what, next time we'll try a Western. Remind me not to let you turn on *Star Trek*."

"*Star Trek*'s a classic," he said, and sent her into a fit of giggles.

"Never mind. You know, I almost think I'm losing my grip. I spent the morning in a spaceship and the afternoon eating pizza and not watching a movie. I don't seem to be able to make sense of it all."

"It'll come clear." He touched his glass to hers before settling his arm around her shoulders. It was comforting, the glow of the lamplight, the warmth of the brandy, the scent of the woman. His woman, Cal thought, if for only a moment. "I like this better than the movies. Tell me about Liberty Stone."

"There's not much."

"Tell me, so I can take it with me."

"I was born here, as I told you before."

"In the bed I sleep in."

"Yes." She sipped her brandy, wondering if it was that, or the image of him in the old bed, that warmed her. "My mother used to weave. Blankets, wall hangings, rugs. She would sell them to supplement what my father grew in the garden."

"They were poor?"

"No, they were children of the sixties."

"I don't understand."

"It's difficult to explain. They wanted to be closer to the land, closer to themselves. It was their part of a revolution against material power, world violence, the entire social structure of the time. So we lived here and my mother bartered and sold her work in the surrounding towns. One day an art buyer on a camping trip with his family came across one of her tapestries." She smiled into her brandy. "The rest, as they say, is history."

"Caroline Stone," he said abruptly.

"Why, yes."

With a laugh, he downed the brandy and reached for the bottle in one smooth motion. "Your mother's work is in museums." Bemused, he picked up the corner of the blanket beside them. "I've seen it in the Smithsonian." He poured more brandy in her glass while she gaped at him.

"This gets stranger and stranger." She drank again, letting the brandy influence her sense of unreality. "It's you we need to talk about, you I need to understand. All these questions." Unable to sit any longer, she cupped the snifter in both hands and started to pace. "The oddest ones pop into my mind. I keep remembering you spoke of Philadelphia and Paris. Do you know what that means?"

"What?"

"We made it." She lifted the snifter in a toast, then recklessly drained it. "It's still there, all of it. Somehow, no matter how close we came to blowing everything, we survived. There's a Philadelphia in the future, Hornblower, and that's the most wonderful thing I can imagine."

Still laughing, she spun in a circle. "All these years I've been studying the past, trying to understand human nature, and now I've had a glimpse of tomorrow. I don't know how to thank you."

Just looking at her left his stomach in a knot. Her cheeks were flushed with excitement. Her body was long and slim and wonderfully graceful as she moved. Wanting her was no longer an urge, it was an obsession.

He drew a long, careful breath. "Glad I could help."

"I want to know everything, absolutely everything. How people live, how they feel. How they court and make love and marry. What games do the children play?" She leaned over to pour another inch of brandy in her glass. "Are hot dogs still the best bet at a baseball game? Are Mondays still the hardest day of the week?"

"You'll have to make a list," he told her. He wanted to keep her talking, moving, laughing. Watching her now, animated, bursting with enthusiasm and humor, was as arousing as being in her arms. "What I can't answer, the computer can."

"A list. Of course. I make terrific lists." Her eyes glowed as she laughed at him. "I know there are more important things for me to ask. Nuclear disarmament, world peace, a cure for cancer and the common cold. But I want to know it all, from the inconsequential to the shattering." Impatiently she pushed her hair back from her face. Her words couldn't seem to keep up with her thoughts. "Every second I think of something new. Do people still have Sunday picnics? Have we beaten world hunger and homelessness? Do all men in your time kiss the way you do?"

The snifter paused halfway to his lips. Very slowly, very deliberately, he set it down. "I can't answer that, because I've only practiced on women."

"I don't know where that came from." She, too, set the snifter aside, then rubbed her suddenly damp palms on the thighs of her jeans. "I suppose I'm a bit wired."

"Excuse me?"

"Nervous, excited. Confused." She pushed her hands through her hair. "Oh, God, Caleb, you confuse me. Even before…before all this."

"We're even there, Libby."

She stared at him. He hadn't moved, but she saw that he had tensed. "That's odd," she murmured. "I don't usually confuse anyone. Nothing seems to be exactly the way I expect it to be with you. I guess I'm a coward, because every time you come near me I want to run."

She closed her eyes. "That's not true. You asked me once if I was afraid of you, and I said I wasn't. That's not true, either. I am afraid. Of you, of me, and most of all of thinking I might never feel this way again with anyone else." She began to roam the room again, picking up a pillow, tossing it aside, shifting a lamp. "I wish I knew what to do, what to say. I don't have any experience with this kind of thing. And, damn it, I wish you'd kiss me again and shut me up."

He thought he could feel each separate nerve in his body stretch. "Libby, you know I want you. I haven't kept it to myself. But under the circumstances…the fact that I'll be gone in a few days…"

"That's just it." Suddenly she wanted to weep. "You will be gone. I don't want to wonder what it might have been like. I want to know. I feel…oh, I don't know how I feel. The only thing I'm sure of is that I want you to make love with me tonight."

She stopped, shocked that she had said it aloud, stunned that it was perhaps the truest thing she'd ever said. Then the nerves were gone, and the shock with them. She was absolutely calm, and absolutely certain.

"Caleb, I want to be with you tonight."

He rose. The hands he tucked in his pockets were two tense fists. "A few days ago it would have been easy. Things have changed, Libby. I care about you."

"You care, so you don't want to love me?"

"I want to so badly I can taste it." When his gaze whipped to hers, she could see that he spoke nothing less than the truth. "I also know that you've had a little too much to drink and more than too much to deal with tonight." He didn't dare touch her, but his voice was like a caress. "There are rules, Libby."

She took what she knew might be the biggest step in her life when she moved to him and held out both hands.

"Break them."

Chapter 7

He could hear his own heart beating, could feel the blood pumping to and from it. In the shadowy light she looked mysterious, impossibly erotic in a baggy sweater and worn corduroy. Her hair was mussed, from the drive and from her own restless fingers. He could imagine, all too clearly, what it would be like to smooth it himself. How it would be to slip off all those layers of oversize clothing and find her slim and warm underneath. He took a long, careful breath and tried to think clearly.

"Libby..." He ran a hand over his roughened chin. "I'm trying to think like a man you'd understand, one from your time. I don't seem to be doing a good job of it."

"I'd rather you'd think like yourself." She wanted to be calm and confident. This was a decision she'd waited years to make. She was sure. But still there were nerves, brought on by excitement, anticipation and deep-rooted doubts about her own capabilities as a woman. "Time doesn't change everything, Caleb."

"No." He was certain men had felt this stirring since the first dawn. But when he looked at her he was afraid that what he was feeling was far more complicated than basic attraction. His throat was dry, his palms were damp. The harder he tried to think rationally, the less clear his thoughts became. "Maybe we should talk about it."

She resisted the urge to stare at her feet and kept her eyes on his. "Don't you want me?"

"I've imagined making love with you a dozen times."

She felt the thrill, and the fear, tangle in a race up her spine. "When you imagined, where were we?"

"Here. Or in the forest. Or thousands of miles away in space. There's a pond near my house, with water as clear as glass and a bank of flowers my father planted. I've seen you there with me."

It hurt, more than a little, knowing he would go back to that pond, to a place where she couldn't follow. But they had now. The present was all that mattered, all she would let matter. She crossed to him, knowing that they both needed for her to take the first step.

"Here's a good start." She lifted a hand to his cheek. "Kiss me again, Caleb."

How could he resist her? He was certain no man could. Her eyes were huge and dark, her lips were parted. Waiting. Slowly he lowered his, just brushing, testing. Her soft, yielding sigh seemed to fill him. Need did, a wild, urgent need. Shaken by the scope of it, he put his hands on her shoulders to draw her away.

"Libby—"

"Don't make me seduce you," she murmured. "I don't know how."

With a strangled laugh, he pulled her hard against him, burying his face in her hair. "Too late. You already have."

"Have I?" Her arms were around him, holding tight to what she told herself she would release without regret when the time came. A shudder had her gripping harder when he caught her earlobe between his teeth. "I don't know what to do next."

Cal plucked her up into his arms. "Enjoy," he told her before he carried her up the stairs.

He wanted her in the bed where he'd dreamed of her. In the pale light of the rising moon he laid her down. Whatever he had he would give her. What she had he would take. He understood pleasure, the degrees, the depths, the layers. Soon, very soon, so would she.

Slowly he undressed her, drawing out the process

for his own enjoyment and for the simple wonder of it. Every inch he uncovered delighted him, the slender ankles, the smooth calves, the curving shoulders. He watched her eyes widen and cloud with confused passions when he touched her, palms skimming, fingers trailing.

Taking her hand, he brought it to his mouth to taste and savor. "I've seen you like this," he murmured. "Even when I tried not to."

She'd thought she would feel awkward, even foolish. She lay naked in the splash of moonlight and felt only beautiful as he looked his fill. "I've wanted to be here with you, even when I tried not to." She was smiling when she lifted her hands to undress him.

He was determined to be patient, to be thorough, to be very, very gentle. He knew, as he understood she did not, that there were hundreds of varied paths to fulfillment. This time, her first time, it would be sweet. Then her inexperienced hands made his blood leap under his skin. Seduction, unplanned, was potent. Once he covered her hands with his and bit back a moan.

Her fingers tightened under his, and her body tensed. "Am I doing something wrong?"

"No." He let out his breath on a quick laugh and forced himself to relax. "A little too right. This time." Shifting away, he slipped out of the rest of his clothes. "Remind me to ask you to undress me like that again later." He brushed her hair back from her face and began to kiss her. "This first time I have things to show you, places to take you." He nipped lightly at her chin. "Trust me."

"I do." But she was already trembling. The brush of his body against hers, warmth to warmth, was like some strange, exciting dream. His hands roamed over her, whisper-soft, limber as a violinist's, and a knot of heat built from her center out to her fingertips before she could do more than wrap her arms around him. She melted into the kiss, into the long, luxurious depth of it. Then those clever fingers found a point, some pulse that beat under the skin near the base of her spine, and sent her reeling.

His mouth muffled her cry of stunned release as her body arched, then went as fluid as water beneath his. Almost experimentally, he eased her up and over again, his own body vibrating from her pleasure.

"Incredible," he murmured before she dragged his mouth back to hers.

Her response had his blood pounding. She was like a fast fuse, and he held the still-smoking match. He knew that if he had taken her that instant she would have welcomed him, just as he knew desire was only the root of the flower. He wanted to give her the blossom.

Delving deep, he found the control that he needed to prolong passion rather than be commanded by it. She seemed so fragile now, her taste, her scent, the liquid movements she made under him. Like the moonbeams that washed the room, she was pale and beautiful. With his lips against her throat, he could feel her pulse thunder, echoing his own.

No fantasy he had ever indulged in, no woman he had ever pleasured, had been as glorious as the woman who held him now. He linked a hand with hers, knowing he would never find the words to explain to either of them what this night with her meant to him.

But he could show her. He would show her.

One moment she was floating, the next racing. Then she was flying. Love with him was a myriad of tastes and textures, a storm of sensations, a symphony of sounds. His hands were almost unbearably gentle, and the scrape of his beard against her skin was an arousing contrast. As she gave herself the liberty of touching him, of stroking him, she discovered that his body was wire-taut and his muscles were trembling.

She wanted to think, to analyze each moment, but it was possible only to experience.

Soft, so incredibly soft…she was almost afraid it was an illusion, his touch, the words he murmured, the glow that seemed to surround her. Then there was heat, stunningly real. She was steeped in it. In him.

He lifted her so that they were kneeling in the center of the bed, wrapped close. Flickers of urgency came through…a roughened caress, a quickened breath. A skim of fingers, a press of pulse to pulse, and he had her gasping, her head thrown back, her body curved against his. He groaned and crushed his hungry mouth to her throat.

Her nails bit into his skin. Even that aroused him. Here was passion, wilder, freer than any he had ever imagined. She was open for him, only him. He was half-mad with the knowledge that she would give to him what she had given to no one else.

But gently. Dragging himself back, he eased his possessive grip into a caress. When he lowered his mouth to her breast, the sound of pleasure came from both of them. He used his tongue to tease, his teeth to torment. He could feel her skin hum under his hands and lips.

She was small, delicate. It helped to bring out the tenderness he wanted to show her. But when he laid her back there was a strength and demand in the hands that pressed him against her.

So long. The thought raced in and out of her mind as he did things to her, for her, things she had never imagined. She had waited so long for this. For him. Her response came freely and fully, her loving of him totally instinctive. There was no way for her to know as she spun in the world he had opened for her what she brought to him.

He was skilled, and he used his skill to take her beyond those first flashes of pleasure into the velvet space reserved for lovers. She was innocent, yet, just as truly, just as easily, she took him. He slipped into her. She closed around him.

It was a merging of bodies, and of hearts, and of time.

Clouds. Dark, silver-edged clouds. Libby was floating on one. She wanted to go on drifting forever. Her arms had slid from around him, limp, to lie on the rumpled sheets. She couldn't find the strength to lift them and encircle him again. Nor could she find her voice. She wanted to tell him not to move—not ever to move. With her eyes closed and his body fitted so perfectly against hers, she counted each beat of his heart.

Silk. Her skin was like hot, fragrant silk. He was certain he could never get enough of it. With his face buried in her hair, he felt his system drift back to earth like a feather on the breeze. How could he tell her that no one had ever moved him as she did? How could he explain that at this moment he was more at home than he had ever been in his own world, or in the sky he loved so much? How could he accept that he had found his match in a place, and in a time, where he was a stranger?

He wouldn't think of it. Cal turned his lips into her neck. For as long as it was possible, he would live from minute to minute.

"You are so lovely." He propped himself on an elbow so that he could see her face, the paleness of it in the moonlight. It was flushed from the afterglow of love-making. Her eyes were clouded with the last dregs of spent passion. "Very lovely," he murmured, and kissed her. "Your skin's still warm." He began to nibble, as though she were a delicacy he couldn't resist.

"I don't think I'll ever be cold again." Fresh desire began to tingle within her. "Caleb—" Her breath caught on a fast, hot shudder. "You make me feel…"

"How?" With his tongue, he traced her parted lips. "Tell me how I make you feel."

"Magical." Her fingers curled into the sheets. "Help-less." And went lax. "Strong." She gripped his fore-arms, rocked by a dazzling array of new sensations. "I don't know."

"I'm going to love you again, Libby." He crushed his mouth to hers in a soul-wrenching kiss that left them both breathless. "And again, and again. Each time I do, it'll be different."

There was a power building in him. It might have frightened her if she hadn't felt its twin growing in her. Her eyes stayed open and on his as she lifted her arms and rose to meet him.

Limbs entwined, they lay together in the deepest part of the night and listened to the wind rising through the trees. He was right, Libby thought. Each time was different, excitingly different, yet beautifully the same. She could, she hoped, live out her life on the memories of this one night.

"Are you asleep?"

She settled her head more comfortably in the curve of his shoulder. "No."

"I might enjoy waking you." He slid his hand up to cup her breast. "In fact, I'm sure I would." He nestled his leg cozily between her thighs. "Libby?"

"Yes?"

"Something's missing."

"What?"

"Food."

She smothered a yawn against his shoulder. "You're hungry? Now?"

"I've got to keep up my strength."

A quick, wicked grin curved her lips. "You've been doing pretty well so far."

"Pretty well?" When she chuckled, he pulled her on top of him. "But I'm not finished yet. Why don't I watch while you fix me a sandwich?"

She traced lazy patterns on his chest with her fingertip. "So, male chauvinism survives in the twenty-third century."

"I fixed you breakfast this morning."

She remembered the little silver bag. "More or less."

Had it only been that morning? Could a life change so unalterably in just a few short hours? Hers had. She wondered if that should frighten her, but all she felt was gratitude.

"All right." She started to push away, but then he gripped her hips and shifted her.

"First things first," he murmured, and sent her soaring again.

Later, Libby struggled into a robe, wondering if her mind could handle the simple task of slapping some meat between two slices of bread. He'd drained her and filled her, aroused her and soothed her, until her limbs were weak and her mind was mush.

He switched on the bedside light as he rose out of the bed, unabashedly naked. "Got any cookies to go with that sandwich?"

"Probably." She didn't want to stare at him. Yes, she did. Though she knew it was foolish, her color rose as she lowered her eyes to watch her fingers fumble with the belt of her robe. When he walked toward the door, she looked up quickly. "You're not going downstairs like that."

"Like what?"

"Without… You need to put something on."

He leaned a hand against the doorjamb and grinned. Watching her blush delighted him. "Why? You should know how I'm built by now."

"That's not the point."

"What is the point?"

Giving up, she gestured to the pile of clothes. "Put something on."

"Okay. I'll put on the sweater."

"Very funny, Hornblower."

"You're shy." A glint came into his eyes, one she recognized very well by now. Even as he took the first step toward her, she snatched up the jeans and tossed them at him.

"If you want me to fix you a sandwich, you'll have to cover up some of your…attributes."

Still grinning, he struggled into the jeans. If he put them on, she'd just have to take them off him later. Enjoying the idea, he followed her downstairs.

"Why don't you fill the teakettle?" she suggested as she opened the refrigerator.

"With what?"

"Water," she said with a sigh. "Just water. Put it on the front burner of the stove and turn the little knob under it." She pulled out some packaged ham, some cheese and a hothouse tomato. "Mustard?"

"Hmm?" He was studying the stove. "Sure."

People now had to be very patient, he decided as he watched the electric coil of the burner slowly glow red with heat. Still, there were advantages. Libby's cooking was a far cry from the quick packs he was accustomed to. Then there were the living arrangements. Though he had always loved the home he'd grown up in and was more than comfortable in his quarters aboard his ship, he liked the feel of real wood under his bare feet, and the smell of it burning when she had a fire going in the main room.

Then there was Libby herself. He wasn't certain it was proper to call her an advantage. She was distinct, unique, and everything he'd ever wanted in a woman. His mouth fell open an instant before the heat from the burner singed his finger. With a quick yelp, he jumped back.

"What is it?"

For a moment he just stared at her. Her hair was tousled around her face, and her eyes were heavy from lack of sleep. The robe she wore seemed to swallow her up.

"Nothing," he managed, nearly overwhelmed by an emotion that he prayed was only desire. "I burned my finger."

"Don't play with the stove," she said mildly, then went back to making the sandwiches.

Everything he wanted in a woman? That wasn't possible. He didn't know what he wanted in a woman, and he was a long way from making up his mind. Or had been.

That thought put the fear of God into him. That, and the uncomfortable suspicion that his mind had been made up for him the moment he'd opened his eyes and seen her dozing in the chair. Ridiculous. He hadn't even known her then.

But he knew her now.

He couldn't be in love with her. He watched as she tossed her hair back from her face with a flick of her hand, and his stomach tied itself into knots. Attraction, however outrageous, was acceptable. It wasn't possible that he was in love. He could love being with her, love making love with her, laughing with her. He could care for her, find her fascinating and arousing, but as for love, that wasn't an option.

Love, here and in his time, meant things neither of them could ever have together. A home, a family. Years.

As the kettle began to sputter, he let out a long breath. He was simply magnifying the situation. She was special to him, and always would be. The days he spent with her would be a precious part of his life. But it was essential for him to remember, for both their sakes, that his life began two hundred years after Libby no longer existed.

"Is something wrong?"

He glanced over to see her holding two plates, her head cocked a bit to the side, as it did whenever she was trying to work out a problem.

"No." He smiled and took the plates from her. "My mind was wandering."

"Eat, Hornblower." She patted his cheek. "You'll feel better."

Because he wanted to believe it could be that simple, he sat down and dug in while she fixed the tea.

It seemed natural, Libby thought, for them to share tea and sandwiches in the middle of the night—just the two of them sitting in the cozy kitchen, with an owl hooting somewhere in the forest and the moonlight fading. The awkwardness she had felt—foolishly, she believed—before she'd tugged on her robe, was gone.

"Better?" she asked him when he'd downed half of his sandwich.

"Yes." The tension that had slammed into him so unexpectedly had nearly dissipated. He stretched out his legs so that the arch of his foot rubbed over her ankle. There was something soothing in the contact, like a long nap on a rainy afternoon. She looked so pretty with her hair mussed and her eyes heavy. "How is it," he murmured, "that I'm the first man to have you?"

She nearly choked before she managed to swallow the tea that was halfway down her throat. "I don't…" She coughed a little, then tugged the lapels of her robe closer. "I don't know how to answer that."

"Do you consider that an odd question?" Charmed again, he smiled, leaning closer so that he could touch her hair. "You're so sensitive, so attractive. Other men must have wanted you."

"No...that is, I can't say. I haven't really paid much attention."

"Does it embarrass you for me to tell you you're attractive?"

"No." But when she picked up her teacup with both hands she was flushed. "A little, perhaps."

"I can't be the first to have told you how lovely you are. How warm." He pried one of her hands from the cup to soothe her fingers. "How exciting."

"Yes, you can." Almost unbearably aroused, she let out a long, shaky breath. "I haven't had a lot of...social experience with men. My studies." Her breath snagged as he kissed her fingers. "My work."

He released her hand before he went with his impulse to make love with her again. "But you study men."

"Studying and interacting are different things." He didn't have to touch her to stir her, Libby realized. He only had to look, as he was looking now. "I'm not very outgoing unless I concentrate on it."

He started to laugh, then realized she believed it. "I think you underestimate Liberty Stone. You took me in and cared for me, and I was a stranger."

"I could hardly have left you out in the rain."

"You couldn't. Others could. History may not be my strong suit, Libby, but I doubt human nature has changed that much. You went out in the storm to find me, brought me into your home, let me stay even when

I annoyed you. If I get back to my own time and place it will be because of you."

She rose then to fix more tea she didn't want. She didn't want to think about his leaving, though she knew she would have to. It was wrong to pretend, even for a few hours, that he would stay with her and forget the life he'd left behind.

"I don't think giving you a bed and some scrambled eggs constitutes a real debt." She made herself smile as she turned toward him again. "But if you want to be grateful I won't argue with you."

He'd said something wrong. Though he couldn't put his finger on it, Cal could tell from the way her eyes had changed. She was smiling at him, but her eyes were dark and sad. "I don't want to hurt you, Libby."

Her eyes softened now, and he was relieved. "No, I know that." She sat down again and poured each of them another full cup. "What do you plan to do? About getting back, I mean."

"How much do you know about physics?"

"Next to nothing."

"Then let's just say I'll put the ship's computer to work. The damage was pretty minimal, so that shouldn't be a problem. I'll have to ask you to drive me out to the ship again."

"Of course." She felt a bubble of panic and struggled to get past it. "I suppose you'll want to stay on the ship now, while you work out your calculations and make your repairs."

It would be more practical, and it would certainly be more convenient. Cal gave it no more than a moment's consideration. "I was hoping I could stay here. I've got my aircycle on board, so I can get back and forth easily enough. If you don't mind the company."

"No, of course not." She said it quickly, too quickly, flustering herself. Then she stopped and backed up. "Your aircycle?"

"If it wasn't damaged in the crash," he mused. Then he tossed the possibility aside. "We'll have a look tomorrow. Are you going to eat the rest of that?"

"What? Oh, no." She passed him the second half of her sandwich. It was ridiculous, she supposed, but every now and then he said something that made her wonder if she was dreaming again. "Cal," she began slowly, "it occurs to me that I can never tell anyone about you, or any of this."

"I'd rather you'd wait until I've gone." He finished off the sandwich. "But I don't mind if you tell anyone."

"That's big of you." She gave him a bland look. "Tell me, do they have padded cells in the twenty-third century?"

"Padded cells?" He took a moment to imagine one. "Is that a joke?"

"Only on me," she told him as she rose to clear the plates.

"It may be one on me, too. I've wondered if, once I get back, anyone will believe me."

A thought struck her that was both absurd and fascinating. "Maybe I could do a time capsule. I could write everything down, put in a few interesting or pertinent items and seal it up. We could bury it—I don't know, down by the stream, perhaps. When you got back you could dig it all up."

"A time capsule." The idea appealed to him, not just scientifically, but personally. Wouldn't it mean he would still have something of her, even when they were separated by centuries? He would need that, he realized, the solid proof of not only where he had been but that she had existed. "I can run it through the computer, make sure we don't put it somewhere that's going to be covered by a building or a landslide or some such thing."

"Good." She picked up a pad from the counter and began to scribble.

"What are you doing?"

"Making notes." She squinted at her own writing and wished she had her glasses. "We'll need to write everything down, of course, starting with you and your ship. What else should we put in it?" she wondered, tapping the pencil against the pad. "A newspaper, I think, and a picture would be good. We may have to drive back into town and find one of those little booths that take pictures. No, I'll buy a Polaroid camera." She scribbled faster. "That way we can take pictures here, in the house or right outside. Then we'll need some personal things…" She fingered the thin gold chain at her throat. "Maybe some basic household items."

"You're being a scientist." He took her by the waist and drew her slowly, unerringly, against him. "I find that very exciting."

"That's silly."

But it didn't seem silly at all when he lowered his head and began to nibble at her neck. She felt the floor tilt beneath her feet.

"Cal…"

"Hmm?" He journeyed up to a small, vulnerable spot just behind her ear.

"I wanted to…" The pad slipped out of her hand and landed on the floor at their feet.

"To what?" Quick and clever, his fingers loosened the knot at her waist. "Tonight you can have anything you want."

"You." She sighed as her robe slid off her shoulders. "Just you."

"That's the easy part." More than willing to oblige, he braced her against the counter. A hundred erotic ideas swam through his mind. He was going to see to it that neither of them thought the same way about this cozy little kitchen again. The streaks of pink along her skin stopped him.

"What's all this?" Curious, he ran a finger over the

swell of her breast, then shifted his hand to his chin. "I've scratched you."

"What?" She was already floating an inch off the floor, and she was less than willing to touch down.

"I haven't shaved in days." Annoyed with himself, he bent to lightly kiss the skin he'd irritated earlier. "You're so soft."

"I didn't feel a thing." She reached for him again, but he only kissed her hair.

"There's only one thing to do."

"I know." She ran her hands up his muscled back.

With a laugh, he hugged her tighter. "That's two things." He scooped her up again for no other reason than that it felt wonderful.

"You don't have to carry me." But she nuzzled into his shoulder. "I can walk to bed."

"Maybe, but we'd better use the bathroom for this."

"The bathroom?"

"I'm going to have to deal with that nasty-looking device," he told her as he started up the stairs. "And you're going to walk me through it so I don't cut my throat."

Nasty-looking device? She tried to put it all together as he carried her upstairs. "Don't you know how to use a razor?"

"We're civilized where I come from. All instruments of torture have been outlawed."

"Is that so?" She waited until he set her down again.

"I suppose that means women don't wear high heels or control-top panty hose. Never mind," she said when he opened his mouth. "I think this could become a very philosophical discussion, and it's much too late." Opening the linen closet, she took out the razor and the shaving cream. "Here you go."

"Right." He looked at the tools in his hand with a kind of resigned dread. What a man did for his woman. "Just how do I go about this?"

"This is all secondhand, as I've never shaved my face before, but I believe you spread on the shaving cream, then slide the edge of the razor over your beard."

"Shaving cream." He squirted some into his hand, then ran his tongue over his teeth. "Not toothpaste."

"No, I…" It didn't take her long to get the picture. Leaning back against the sink, she covered her mouth with her hand and tried, unsuccessfully, not to giggle. "Oh, Hornblower, you poor thing."

Cal studied the can in his hand. As he saw it, he really had no choice. While Libby was bent nearly double, he turned, aimed and fired.

Chapter 8

She awakened slowly, muttering a bit when the sunlight intruded on her dreams. She shifted, or tried to, but she was weighed down by an arm around her waist and a leg hooked possessively over hers. Content with that, she snuggled closer and had the pleasure of feeling her sleep-warmed skin rub against Cal's.

She didn't know what time it was, and for perhaps the first time in her life it didn't matter. Morning or afternoon, she was happy to lie curled in bed, dozing the day away, as long as he was with her.

Drifting, nearly dreaming again, she stroked a hand over him. Solid, she thought. He was solid and real and, for the moment, hers. Even with her eyes closed she could see him, every feature of his face, every line of his body. There had never been anyone she had felt belonged so completely to her before. Even her parents, for all their love, all their understanding, had belonged to each other initially. She would always think of them as a unit, first and last. And Sunny... Libby smiled a little as she thought of her sister. Even though she was younger by nearly two years, Sunny had always been independent and her own person—argumentative and daring in ways Libby could never try to emulate.

But Cal... It was true that he had only just appeared in her life, would disappear again all too quickly, but he was hers. His laughter, his temper, his passion...they all belonged to her now. She would keep them, treasure them, long after he was gone.

To love as she did, Libby mused, when every emotion, every word, every look, had to be squeezed into a matter of hours, was both precious and heartbreaking.

He thought he'd been dreaming, but the shape, the texture, the scent of a woman's body were very, very real. Libby's body. Her name was there, his first waking thought. She was pressed against him, a perfect fit even in sleep. The slow, gentle stroke of her hand aroused him in the most exquisite way.

He'd lost count of the times they had moved together during the night, but he knew dawn had been breaking the last time she'd cried out his name. The light had been dim and pearly. He would never forget it. She was like a fantasy, all soft curves, agile limbs and tireless passions. Somewhere along the line he had stopped being the teacher and had been taught.

There was more to loving than the uncountable physical pleasures a man and a woman could offer each other. There was trust and patience, generosity and joy. There was the drugging contentment of falling asleep knowing your partner would be there when you awoke.

Partner. The word floated through his mind. His match. Was it fate or fancy that he had had to travel through time to meet his match?

He didn't want to think of it. Refused to. All he wanted now was to make love with Libby in the sunlight.

He shifted, and before either of them was fully awake, slipped into her. Her soft moan mingled with his own as their lips met. Acceptance. Affection. Arousal. Slowly, drawing out the lazy delight, they moved together, their hands beginning a quiet exploration, the kiss deepening.

"I love you."

He heard her words, a caressing whisper in his mind, and answered them like an echo as his lips began to trace her face.

The admissions shocked neither of them, as they were too dazed by the tumultuous sensations and emotions running through them. She had never spoken those words to another man, nor he to another woman. Before the impact hit home, need had them clinging closer.

Gracefully, gloriously, they took each other to the pinnacle.

Later, he nuzzled down between her breasts, but he was no longer sleeping. Had she said she loved him? And had he told her he loved her? What disturbed him most was that he couldn't be sure if it had happened, or if it had been his imagination, something wished for while his mind was vulnerable with sleep and pleasure.

And he couldn't ask her. Didn't dare. Any answer she would give would hurt. If she didn't love him, it would be like losing part of his heart, of his soul. If she did, it would make leaving her something akin to dying.

It was best, for both of them, to take what they had. He wanted to make her laugh, to see both passion and humor in her eyes, to hear them in her voice. And he would remember. Cal closed his eyes tight. Whatever happened to him, he would always remember.

So would she. He needed to be certain of his place in her memories.

"Come with me." Sliding off the bed, he dragged her with him.

"Where?"

"To the bathroom."

"Again?" Laughing, she tried to snag her robe, but he pulled her into the hall without it. "You don't need another shave."

"Good thing."

"You only cut yourself three or four times. And it's your own fault you used up most of the shaving cream beforehand."

He sent her a wicked grin. "I liked rubbing it all over you better."

"If you're getting ideas about the toothpaste…"

"Maybe later." He lifted her up and into the tub. "For now I'll settle for a shower."

She let out a quick shriek when the cold water hit her. Before she could retaliate or form even a token protest he had joined her, wrapping one arm around her while he adjusted the water temperature with his free hand. He thought he was getting rather good at it.

She took a stream of water in the face, sputtered, started to swear, then found herself caught in a hot, wet, endless kiss.

She'd never experienced anything like it. Steamy air, slick skin, soapy hands. Her knees were weak by the time he shut the spray off and wrapped her in a towel. As dizzy as she, he rested a forehead on hers.

"I think if we're going to get anything done—anything else, that is—we'd better get out of the house."

"Right."

"After we eat."

She was amazed she had the energy to laugh. "Naturally."

* * *

It was late afternoon when they stood by Cal's ship again. Clouds had moved in from the north, bringing a chill. Libby told herself that was the reason she felt cold. She hugged the short jacket tighter, but the cold came from inside.

"I'm standing here, looking at it, knowing it's real, but I still can't understand it."

Cal nodded. His contented, relaxed mood had fled, and he wasn't entirely sure why. "I get the same sensation whenever I look at your cabin." There was a headache building behind his eyes, the kind he knew came from tension. "Look, I know you've got work of your own, and I don't want to hold you up, but would you mind waiting a few minutes while I check the cycle?"

"No." She'd been hoping he'd ask her to stay all day. Masking her disappointment, she smiled at him. "Actually, I'd like to see it."

"I'll be right back."

He opened the hatch and disappeared inside.

He would do that again soon, and for the last time, Libby thought. She had to be prepared for it. Strange, but she'd imagined he'd told her he loved her that morning. It was a nice, soothing thought, though she understood he didn't really. He couldn't. He cared for her, more than anyone had ever cared for her, but he hadn't fallen deeply, completely in love with her, as she had with him.

Because she loved him, she was going to do everything she could to help him, starting with accepting limitations. It was a beautiful day, after the most beautiful night of her life. Smiling, really smiling, she looked up at the cloudy sky. The rain would come by evening, and it would be welcome.

She glanced back at the ship when she heard a low, metallic hum. Another door opened—the cargo door, she assumed because of its size and location. Her mouth dropped open as Cal, on the back of a small, streamlined bike, raced out, six inches above the ground.

It made a sound that was something like a purr, not catlike or motorlike, more like the sound of air parting. It was shaped something like a motorcycle, but without the bulk. There were two wheels for ground transportation, and a narrow, padded seat to accommodate riders. The body itself was a long, curving cylinder that forked into two slender handlebars.

He drove—or flew—it over to her, then sat grinning on the seat like a ten-year-old showing off his first twelve-speed.

"It runs great." He made some small movement with his hand on the handgrips that had the purr deepening. "Want a ride?"

Frowning, she eyed the little gauges and buttons on

the stock beneath the handlebars. It looked like a toy. "I don't know."

"Come on, Libby." Wanting to share his pleasure, he held out a hand. "You'll like it. I won't let anything happen to you."

She looked at him, and at the bike, hovering just above the pine needles that were strewn on the forest floor. It was a small machine—if indeed that was the proper term—but there was room enough for two on the narrow black seat. The body was painted a metallic blue that glistened with deeper shades in the sunlight. It looked harmless, she decided after a moment, and she doubted if anything so small could hold much power. With a shrug, she slid on the seat behind him.

"Better hold on," he told her, mostly because he wanted to feel her body curve against his.

The strength of the vibration beneath her shocked her, though she knew it was foolish. Cal had looked harmless, too, she remembered. "Hornblower, shouldn't we have helmets or—" The words whipped away as he accelerated.

She might have screamed, but instead she squeezed her eyes shut and gripped Cal so tightly that he choked on a laugh. He could feel her heart beating against him, as fast and heavy as it had through the night. With an innate skill honed finer by practice, he steered once around the ship, then up the slope.

Speed. He'd always been addicted to it. He felt the air slap his face, stream through his hair, and pressed for more. The sky beckoned, his first and most constant lover, but he resisted, aware that Libby would be more frightened than thrilled if he took her too high too quickly. Instead he breezed through the forest, winding around trees, skimming over rock and water. A bird burst off a branch just above their heads and went wheeling away, chattering bad-temperedly at the competition. He could feel her grip relax a fraction, then a little more. Her face was no longer pressed between his shoulder blades.

"What do you think?"

She could nearly breathe again. It seemed her stomach had decided to stay in place. At least for the moment. She opened one eye for a cautious look. And swallowed hard.

"I think I'm going to murder you the minute we're on the ground again."

"Relax." The cycle tilted thirty degrees right, then left, as he danced through the trees.

Easy for him to say, she thought. Another look showed her that they were more than ten feet above the ground. She gasped, nearly managed to squeal out a demand to be set down, but then it hit her. She was flying. Not enclosed in some huge, bulky plane thousands of feet up, but freely, lightly. She could feel the wind on her face, in her hair, could taste the promise of spring on it. There was no loud roar of engine noise to disturb the sensation. They were skimming through the forest as playfully as birds.

He stopped in the center of the clearing his ship had created. While the bike hovered, he turned to look at her.

"Want me to go down?"

"No. Up." She laughed and tossed her head back. She had already felt the pull of the sky.

He was grinning when he leaned back to kiss her. "How high?"

"What's the limit?"

"I don't know, but I don't think we ought to chance it. If we go up above the trees, somebody might spot us."

He was right, of course. Libby pushed her hair out of her face, wondering why she seemed to have so little sense when she was around him. "To the treetops, then. Just once."

Delighted with her, he turned around. He felt her arms hook firmly around him, and then they were flying again.

He'd never forget. However many times he had taken to sky and space, however many times he would yet take to them, he would never forget this one playful flight with Libby. She was laughing, and the sound of it caressed his ear as her body pressed companionably against his. Her fingers were linked loosely at his waist. His only regret was that he couldn't watch her face as they rose up and up. Making love with her was like this, as clean and clear as cutting through the air. As mystifying and seductive as defying gravity.

He resisted the temptation to crest the trees, contenting himself, and her, with gliding around the thick branches at a hundred feet. Below they could see a thin stream that cut through the rock, and a waterfall, driven by the spring rain and the snowmelt that danced down the ridge and fell into space. The sun pushed through the clouds so that they could watch the pattern of shadows shift on the ground below.

For a moment they both turned their faces to the sky and wished.

He slowed for their descent, and they seemed to drift downward, weightless, soundless. Libby felt her hair lift off her neck, teased by the air currents. She thought pleasantly of Peter Pan and fairy dust before they touched down lightly beside the ship.

"Okay?"

When he turned to look over his shoulder, Libby noticed that the faint hum had stopped. The chill had vanished. "It was wonderful. I could have stayed up all day."

"Flying's habit-forming." No one knew that better

than he. He swung off, then took her hand. "I'm glad you liked it."

It was over, Libby told herself when she felt her feet on solid ground again. But she had one more memory to store away. "I loved it. I'm not going to ask you how it works. I doubt I'd understand anyway, and it might spoil the fun." With her hand still caught in his, she looked at the ship. Her feelings about it were as confused as the rest of her emotions. It had brought him to her, and it would take him away. "I'll let you get to work."

Cal was dealing with the same tug-of-war himself. "I'll be back around nightfall."

"All right." She took her hand from his, then stuck it restlessly in her pocket. "You won't have any trouble finding your way?"

"I'm a good navigator."

"Of course." The birds they had frightened away with their ride were beginning to sing again. Time was slipping by. "Well, I'd better go."

He knew she was stalling, but then, so was he. It was stupid, Cal told himself. He would be with her again in a matter of hours. "You could come in with me, but I don't think I'd get a lot done."

It was tempting. She could go inside, distract him, keep him away from the computer and the answers for a few more hours. But it wouldn't be right. Libby looked up at him again as all the love and the longing welled up inside her.

"I haven't gotten any work done the last couple of days, either."

"All right." Leaning over, he kissed her. "See you tonight."

He stood by the open hatch as she started up the slope. But when she reached the top of the ridge she didn't look back.

Libby spent most of the day drafting an account of the series of events that had occurred over the last week. She used Cal's words, his theory, to explain how he had come to be with her, coloring them with her own impressions. Then she listed, in the orderly fashion that was second nature to her, everything that had happened, from the time she had seen the flash in the sky until she had left Cal beside the ship.

That was the simple part, setting down the facts. Her memory was faultless. She knew that would be both a blessing and a curse when she was alone again. But for now she pulled together her objectivity and gave the story as much skill and dedication as she had her dissertation.

Once done, she read the entire story over twice, refining or enlarging where she saw fit. She was trained to report, she mused as she studied the computer screen.

When Cal presented his experiences to the scientists of his time, she wanted him to have the benefit of whatever skill she could give him.

It was a fantastic story, fantastic in the most literal sense of the word. Perhaps it wouldn't seem quite as fantastic in Cal's time. How would his people react to him when he returned, when he told his tale? The accidental explorer, she thought with a smile. Well, Columbus had been looking for India when he'd discovered the New World.

She liked to think that he would be treated as a kind of hero, that he was a man whose name would be in history books.

He had the look of a hero, she mused, daydreaming a little as her glasses slipped down her nose. Tall and tough. The bandage over his brow added a rakish look—as the week's growth of beard had before he'd shaved it. For her, she remembered, and felt the deep glow of pleasure.

He was, perhaps, an ordinary man in his time. A man, she supposed, who did his job as others did, who groaned over getting up in the morning, one who occasionally drank too much or forgot to pay bills. He wasn't wealthy or brilliant or wildly successful. He was simply Caleb Hornblower, a man who had taken a wrong turn and become extraordinary.

To her, he would never be just a man. He would always be *the* man.

Would she love again? No, Libby thought with the calm of absolute certainty. She would be content, somehow, with her work and her family, with her memories. But to love again would be impossible. She had, even as a child, believed that there would be only one man for her. Perhaps that was why it had always been so easy for her to concentrate on studies and career while her contemporaries had drifted in and out of relationships and fallen in and out of love.

She hated making mistakes. Libby smiled a little reluctantly at the admission. It was a flaw, certainly, one of pride, but she had always detested the idea of taking a misstep, personally or professionally. That was why she studied harder than most, researched more thoroughly, considered more carefully.

It had paid off, she reflected as she pushed a few buttons and had her dissertation flashing onto the screen. She was young for the degree of success she'd achieved. And she intended to achieve a great deal more.

She was old, perhaps, to be having her first love affair. But caution and care hadn't led her astray. Loving Cal would never be a mistake.

Content, she pushed her glasses more securely on her nose, leaned forward and went to work.

He found her there hours later, her posture long forgotten, absorbed in a culture as different from hers as hers was to Cal. She'd switched on the desk lamp at dusk, and the light slanted across her hands.

Strong, capable hands, Cal thought. Probably inherited from her artist mother. The nails were short and unpainted, at the ends of long fingers. There was a scar, a faint one he'd noticed before, along the base of her thumb. He'd meant to ask her how she'd come by it.

He thought he'd been tired when he'd come in—not physically, but mentally, with the burden of figures and calculations weighing on his mind. But now, seeing her, fatigue was forgotten.

He'd managed, somehow, to stop thinking about her while he'd worked. It had been a deliberate effort to stop thinking, stop wanting, stop needing. Because of it, he'd managed to make some progress. He was all but sure of what he had to do to get home. He knew the odds and the risks. Now, watching her, he knew the sacrifice.

He'd only known her briefly. It was necessary, very necessary, to remind himself of that. His life wasn't here, with her. He had a home, an identity. He had a family, he realized now, that he loved more than he had once comprehended.

But he stood and watched her as the minutes ticked away, absorbing every breath, every careless gesture. The way her hair swept over her neck, the way her stockinged foot tapped impatiently when her fingers paused. Now and then she would drag a hand through her hair or cup her chin in her palms and stare owlishly at the screen. He found every movement endearing. When he finally said her name, his voice was strained.

"Libby."

She jolted and spun in her chair to stare at him. The hallway was dark behind him. He was just a silhouette, propped casually against the door frame. Love nearly smothered her.

"Oh. I didn't hear you come in."

"You were pretty deep in your work."

"I guess." When he stepped into the room, the intensity in his eyes had her drawing her brows together. "What about yours? Did it go well?"

"Yes."

"You look upset. Is something wrong?"

"No." He reached down to touch her face, and his eyes softened. "No."

"Your calculations?"

"Coming along." Her skin felt like silk, he thought, and it warmed under his touch. "In fact, I made more progress than I'd expected."

"Oh." He thought he saw a shadow flicker in her eyes, but her voice was bright and encouraging. "That's good. Did you ride the cycle back?"

"Yeah. I left it behind the shed."

It had been a stupid question, she thought. He would hardly have hiked all the way. She wanted to ask him to take her up again, now, while the moon was rising. The wind was already picking up, warning of rain. It would be wonderful. But he looked tired, and troubled.

"Well, after all that you must be hungry." She glanced around as if noticing the dark for the first time. "I hadn't realized it was so late. Why don't I go down and toss something together?"

"It can wait." Taking her hand, he drew her to her feet. The machine continued to hum, forgotten by both of them. "We can go down later and both throw something together. I like the way you look in glasses."

With a quick laugh, she reached for them. He caught her hand so that both of hers were trapped in his.

"No, don't take them off." He tilted his head to kiss her, as if experimenting. Her taste was the same. Thank God. Most of the tension dissolved. "They make you look…smart and serious."

Though her heart was already thumping, she smiled. "I am smart and serious."

"Yes, I suppose you are." He ran his thumbs over the inside of her wrists and felt her pulse scramble. "The way you look right now makes me want to see just how unintellectual I can make you." With their hands still joined, he bent to kiss her, holding himself back, teasing and nibbling her lips until her breath was a shudder.

"Libby?"

"Yes."

"What can you tell me about the mudmen of New Guinea?"

"Nothing." She strained against him, moaning a bit when his lips continued to brush, featherlight, over hers. "Nothing at all. Kiss me, Caleb."

"I am." His lips cruised over her face, skimming here, lingering there. She was like a volcano, awakened after eons of sleep, ready to burst free, hot and molten. "Touch me."

"I will."

It was never what she expected. He had her teetering on the edge with only a stroke of his hands. Then, as she trembled back to earth, he began to undress her, peeling off her flannel shirt, tugging off her jeans, while they stood beside the bed. She wore a narrow white undershirt in plain cotton. It seemed to fascinate him as he toyed with the straps, skimmed his finger along the low scooped neck, before he slipped it up and over her head. His lips were never still, nor were his hands, which roamed to exploit all the secrets he'd already discovered.

Delighted, delirious, she yanked his sweater over his head. It amazed her that the need could have sharpened and grown, outracing what she had felt for him the first time. Now she knew where he would take her and had already traveled some of the routes he navigated so expertly.

His skin was soft, smooth. It pleased her to run her hands up and over his back to feel it and the hard muscle beneath. The contrast, the peculiarly masculine contrast, made her knees weak. She heard his breath quicken as she stroked her hands from shoulder to waist.

To be wanted this...desperately. She could feel it in the way he touched her, in the way his mouth came back to hers again and again for longer, deeper, hungrier kisses. His tongue tangled with hers, enticing, erotic, and she felt as well as heard him suck in his breath as her knuckles grazed his stomach.

She had learned, Cal thought dizzily. And she had learned quickly. Her hands, and the gentle movements of her body against his, were driving him beyond reason. He wanted to tell her to give him a moment, to give him the time he needed to gain a firm, lasting grip on control. But it was already too late. Much too late.

He dragged her to the bed. Her gasp of surprise ended in a dark moan of pleasure. She reached for him, only to find herself gripping the bedclothes as he whipped her over the first raw edge.

She'd thought she knew what loving was. Even a night steeped in it hadn't prepared her for this. He was crazed, and in a moment her madness matched his.

No gentle touch, no easy persuasion. It was all hot, ripe need and a desperate race for satisfaction. Like two lost souls, they rolled over the sheets and drowned in each other.

A desperate demand. A fervent answer. Murmured requests were for the sane. Tonight there were only breathless moans and shuddering sighs. Her skin was so slick with the heat passion pumped into her that it slid sleekly over his. Each time his mouth found hers she tasted the rich, musky flavor of desire.

There were no velvet clouds now, but a storm breaking. Exciting. Electric. She could almost hear the air singing with it. Drums seemed to pound inside her head, inside her heart, beating in an ever-increasing rhythm. Gulping in air, she rolled over him to press her open mouth to his throat, his chest, knowing only that his flavor was dark, rich and wonderful.

He couldn't get enough. No matter how much she gave, he needed more and still more. He was unaware that his fingers were digging hard into her skin, bruising, even as his lips followed the trail. He could see her in the dim lamplight, the way her damp skin glowed, the way her head fell back each time pleasure overtook her. Her eyes were gold, like some dark, ancient coin. Tribute for a goddess. He thought of her as one now, as she rose over him, her body curved back like a bow, the light casting an aura around her hair.

He thought he would die for her, thought he would die without her. Then she was taking him into her, deeply, fully. He reached blindly, as she did, and their hands linked.

Then there was no thought at all.

He held her close long after the tremors had subsided in both of them. He tried to remember what he had done, what she had done, but it was all a blur of torrential sensations and emotions that had bordered on the violent. He was afraid he had hurt her, that now that her mind and body had cooled she would pull away from him and what was inside him.

"Libby?"

Her only answer was a slight shifting of her head against his chest. One of her greatest pleasures was feeling his heart race under her cheek.

"I'm sorry." He stroked her hair, wondering if it was too late for tenderness.

Her eyes opened. Even that effort was almost more than she could manage. There was a flicker of doubt she struggled to ignore. "You are?"

"Yes. I don't know what happened. I've never treated another woman like that."

"You haven't?" He couldn't see the smile that curved her lips.

"No." Cautious, ready to release her if she jerked away, he lifted her head. "I'd like to make it up to you," he began. Then saw that the glint in her eyes was not tears but laughter. "You're smiling."

"How," she said, kissing the bandage on his forehead, "would you like to make it up to me?"

"I thought I'd hurt you." He rolled her over on her back, then took a good long look. She was still smiling, and her eyes were dark with centuries of secrets only women fully understood. "I guess not."

"You haven't answered my question." She stretched, not because she meant to entice, but because she felt as contented as a cat in a sunbeam. "How are you going to make it up to me?"

"Well…" He glanced around the rumpled bed, then shimmied up to look down at the floor. Reaching down, he plucked up her fallen glasses. He twirled them once by the sidepiece, then grinned. "Why don't you put these on, and I'll show you?"

Chapter 9

Libby was lingering over a second cup of coffee, wondering if being in love was directly connected to the difficulty she was having facing a day cooped up with her computer. She recognized the signs of procrastination in Cal, as well. He sat across from her, poking at the remains of her breakfast. He'd already eaten his own.

More than procrastination, she mused. He looked troubled again, as he had when he'd come back the night before. As he had seemed, she thought, when they'd fallen asleep. More than once during the night, and the morning, she'd been certain he was about to tell her something. Something she was afraid she would hate to hear.

She wanted to find a way to encourage him, to

smooth the way to his leaving her. Love, she thought with a sigh, had made her crazy.

The rain had come, in a long, quiet shower that had lasted almost until morning. Now, with the sun, the light was soft, ethereal, and there were pockets of mist hugging the ground.

It was a good day for making excuses, for taking aimless walks in the woods, for making lazy love under a quilt. But thinking like that, Libby reminded herself, wouldn't help Cal find his way home.

"You'd better get started." It was a gentle nudge, offered without enthusiasm.

"Yeah." He would rather have sat where he was, ignoring reality. Instead, he stood and, giving her a quick kiss, walked to the back door. When he opened it, the kitchen filled with birdsong. "I was thinking I'd take a break during the afternoon. Maybe come back for lunch. I'm getting so I can't stomach the stores on the ship." It was more that he couldn't stand being away from her, but she smiled, taking him at his word.

"Okay." Already the day seemed brighter. "If I'm not slaving over a hot stove, I'll be upstairs working."

It seemed so normal, Libby thought when he closed the door behind him, to part in the morning with an easy kiss and plans to meet for lunch. That was probably best, she decided after she topped off her cup and took it upstairs with her. There was certainly little else about their relationship that anyone would have called normal.

She worked well into the afternoon, blaming her edginess on the caffeine. She didn't want to dwell on the fact that Cal had seemed too quiet, too thoughtful, that morning. They both had a lot on their minds. And, she reminded herself, he would be back soon. Since it would be a habit soon broken, she decided to cut her own work short to go down and fix him something special for lunch. When she reached the base of the stairs, she heard the sound of a car.

Visitors weren't just rare at the cabin, they were non-existent. Feeling equal parts surprise and annoyance, she opened the front door.

"Oh, my God." Now it was all surprise, with a healthy dose of trepidation. "Mom! Dad!" Then it was love, waves of it, as she rushed out to greet her parents. They stepped out from either side of a small, battered pickup.

"Liberty." Caroline Stone welcomed her daughter with a throaty laugh and a theatrical spread of her arms. She was dressed almost identically to Libby, in faded jeans and a chunky, hip-grazing sweater. But, unlike Libby's plain red wool, Caroline's was a symphony of hues and tones she had woven herself. She wore two jet-black drop earrings—in the same ear—and a necklace of tourmaline that glittered in the light.

Libby kissed Caroline's smooth, unpowdered cheek. "Mom! What are you doing here?"

"I used to live here," she reminded Libby, then kissed her again while William stood back and grinned. They were two of the three most important women in his life. Though they were a generation apart, he noted with pride that his wife looked hardly older than his daughter. Their coloring and build was so similar that more often than not they were mistaken for sisters.

"What am I?" he demanded. "Part of the scenery?" He spun Libby around for one of his hard, swaying hugs. "My baby," he said, and gave her a loud, smacking kiss. "The scientist."

"My daddy," she responded in kind, "the executive."

He winced just a little. "Don't let it get around. So, let me get a look at you."

Grinning, Libby took her own survey. He still wore his hair too long to be conservative, though there was a sprinkle of silver in the dark blond waves, and a bit more dashed through his beard. Both were trimmed now by a barber with a French accent, but little else about William Stone had changed. He was still the man she remembered, the man who had carried her papoose-style through the forest.

He was tall, and at best he would be considered stringy. Long legs and arms gave him a gangly look.

His face was gaunt, his cheekbones sunken. His eyes were a deep, pure gray that promised honesty.

"So?" Libby turned in a saucy circle. "What do you think?"

"Not too bad." He slipped an arm around Caroline's shoulders. Together they looked as they always had. United. "We did a pretty good job on the first two, Caro."

"You did an excellent job," Libby corrected. Then she stopped. "First two?"

"You and Sunbeam, love." With an easy smile, Caroline reached in the back of the pickup. "Why don't we get the groceries inside?"

"But I— Groceries." Biting her lip, Libby watched her parents pull out bags. Several bags. She had to tell them…something. "I'm so happy to see both of you." She grunted a bit when her father set two heavy brown sacks in her arms. "And I'd like to…that is, I should tell you that I'm not…alone."

"That's nice." Absently William pulled out another sack. He wondered if his wife had noticed the bag of barbecued potato chips he'd stashed inside. Of course she had, he thought. She never missed anything. "We always like to meet your friends, baby."

"Yes, I know, but this one—"

"Caro, take that one along inside. One's enough for you to carry."

"Dad." Seeing no other way, Libby blocked her father's progress. She snagged her lip again when she heard the door swing open and shut behind her mother. "I really should explain." Explain what, she wondered? And how?

"I'm listening, Libby, but these bags are getting heavy." He shifted them. "Must be all the tofu."

"It's about Caleb."

That caught his attention. "Caleb who?"

"Hornblower. Caleb Hornblower. He's…here," she managed weakly. "With me."

William cocked one gently arched brow. "Oh, really?"

The man in question parked his cycle behind the shed and, lecturing himself, strode toward the house. There was nothing wrong in taking an afternoon break. In any case, the computer was hard at work even in his absence. He'd completed most of the major repairs to the ship, and in another day, two at the most, it would be ready for flight.

If he wanted to spend an extra hour or so with a beautiful, exciting woman, he was entitled. He wasn't dragging his heels. He wasn't in love with her.

And the sun revolved around the planets.

Swearing under his breath, he walked through the open back door. Just seeing her made him smile. Even if he could only see her small, nicely rounded bottom as she rummaged in the bottom of the refrigerator. His mood lifting, he walked quietly over to grab her firmly, intimately, by the hips.

"Babe, I can never make up my mind which side of you I like best."

"Caleb!"

The astonished exclamation came not from the woman he'd only just turned into his arms but from the kitchen doorway. His head whipped around, and he stared at Libby, who was gaping, wide-eyed, from across the room, her arms full of brown bags. Beside her stood a tall, thin man who was eyeing him with obvious dislike.

Slowly Caleb turned back to see that he was embracing an equally attractive, if somewhat older, woman than the one he'd expected.

"Hello," she said, and smiled quite beautifully. "You must be Libby's friend."

"Yes." He managed to clear his throat. "I must be."

"You might want to let go of my wife," William told him. "So that she can close the refrigerator."

"I beg your pardon." He took a long and very hasty step back. "I thought you were Libby."

"Are you in the habit of grabbing my daughter by the—"

"Dad." Libby cut him off as she dumped the bags on

the table. As beginnings went, she thought, this one was hardly auspicious. "This is Caleb Hornblower. He's… staying with me for a while. Cal, these are my parents, William and Caroline Stone."

Terrific. Since he didn't think he could manage to have his molecules reappear in a different location, he figured he'd better face the music. "Nice to meet you." He found that the best place for his hands was his pockets. "Libby looks a great deal like you."

"So I've been told." Caroline beamed another smile at him. "Though never quite in that way." Wanting to let him off the hook, she offered him a hand. "Will, why don't you put those bags down and say hello to Libby's friend?"

He took his time about it. William wanted to size the man up. Good-looking enough, he supposed. Strong features, steady eyes. Time would tell. "Hornblower, is it?" William was pleased that Cal's grip was cool and firm.

"Yes." It was the first time he'd been weighed and measured so thoroughly since he'd enlisted in the ISF. "Should I apologize again?"

"Once was probably enough." But William held his opinion on the rest in reserve.

"I was just about to make lunch." She had to do something, Libby thought, to keep everyone busy until she'd worked out a solution.

"Good idea." Caroline pulled fresh cauliflower out of a bag. She'd found the chips, and a jar of pickled hot sausages William had smuggled in. "But I'll make it. Why don't you give me a hand, William?"

"But I—"

"Brew some tea," she suggested.

"I'd love some tea," Libby said, knowing it was a sure way to her father's heart. She took Cal by the hand. "We'll be right back." The moment they were in the living room, she turned on him. "What are we going to do?"

"About what?"

With a sound of disgust, Libby paced toward the fireplace. "I've got to tell them something, and it can hardly be that you've just dropped in from the twenty-third century."

"No, I'd just as soon you didn't."

"But I never lie to them." Torn, Libby poked a charred log with her toe. "I can't."

He walked over to cup her chin in his hand. "Leaving out a few small details isn't lying."

"Small details? Like the fact that you came visiting in a spaceship?"

"For one."

She closed her eyes. It should be funny. Maybe it would be in five or ten years. "Hornblower, this situation would be awkward enough without the added bonus of you being from where—make that *when*—you are."

"What situation?"

She tried not to grind her teeth. "They're my parents, this is their house, and you and I are—" She made a circling gesture with her hand.

"Lovers," he supplied.

"Will you keep your voice down?"

Patient, he laid his hands on her shoulders, gently kneading. "Libby, they probably figured that out when I almost kissed your mother in the refrigerator."

"About that—"

"I thought she was you."

"I know. Still—"

"Libby, I realize it wasn't the most traditional way to meet your parents, but I think that of the four of us I was the most surprised."

She couldn't help chuckling. "Maybe."

"Absolutely. So I think we should just get on to the next step."

"Which is?"

"Lunch."

"Hornblower." With a sigh, she dropped her forehead on his chest. It was a pity this was one of the things she loved about him—his ability to appreciate the simple things. "I wish you'd get it through your head that this is a sensitive situation. What are we going to do about it?" She waited one beat. "If you ask me about what, I'm going to smack you."

"You talk tough." Framing her face with his hands, he lifted it. "Let's see some action."

Libby didn't make even a token protest as his mouth lowered to hers. It was all some sort of a dream anyway, she told herself. Surely she could make everything come out all right in her own dream.

There was a loud, annoyed cough from behind her. Jerking away from Cal, she looked at her father. "Ah..."

"Your mother says lunch is ready." Though he hated acting so predictably, he gave Cal one last measuring look before he went back into the kitchen.

"I think he's warming up to me," Cal mused.

In the kitchen, William scowled at his wife. "That man always has his hands on one of my women."

"One of your women." Caroline let out a long, robust laugh. "Really, Will." She tossed her head so that both of her earrings danced. "He does have very nice hands."

"Looking for trouble?" With one arm, he scooped her up against him.

"Always." She gave him a warm and very provocative kiss before turning toward the doorway. "Come sit down," she said, sharing her radiant smile with Cal. "I just threw a salad together."

She had four bowls set out on her own woven mats. In the center of the table was a concoction of vegetables and herbs, with the surprising addition of green bananas, sprinkled with whole-wheat croutons and ready to be mixed with a yogurt dressing. Libby gave one wistful thought to the BLTs she'd planned on before she sat down.

"So, Cal…" Caroline passed him the bowl. "Are you an anthropologist?"

"No, I'm a pilot," he said, just as Libby announced, "Cal's a truck driver."

Libby muttered under her breath as Cal calmly dished up salad. "Cargo," he explained, pleased that he could honor Libby's wish to stick with the truth. "I deal primarily with cargo. Libby figures that makes me an airborne truck driver."

"You fly?" William drummed his long, skinny fingers on the table.

"Yes. That's all I ever really wanted to do."

"It must be exciting." Caroline leaned forward, always willing to be fascinated. "Sunbeam, our other daughter, is taking flying lessons. Maybe you can give her some pointers."

"Sunny's always taking lessons." There was both amusement and affection in Libby's voice as she passed the salad on to her mother. "She's good at everything. She took up parachuting and figured the next step was to learn how to fly the plane herself."

"Makes sense." He glanced over at Caroline. Caroline

Stone, he thought, not for the first time. The twentieth-century genius. Cal would have found it no more incredible to be sharing a meal with Vincent Van Gogh or Voltaire. "This is a wonderful salad, Mrs. Stone."

"Caroline. Thanks." She slanted a look at her husband, knowing he would have preferred his sausages and chips and a cold beer. After more than twenty years, she hadn't quite converted him. That never stopped her from trying.

"I feel very strongly that proper nutrition is what keeps the mind clear and open," she began. "I recently read a study where proper diet and exercise was directly linked to longer life spans. If we cared for ourselves better, we could live well over a hundred years."

Noting the expression on Cal's face, Libby gave his ankle a kick under the table. She had a feeling he'd been about to inform her mother that people did live over the century mark, and regularly.

"What's the use of living that long if you have to eat leaves and twigs?" William began, but then he noted his wife's narrowed look. "Not that these aren't great leaves."

"You can have something sweet for dessert." She leaned over to kiss his cheek. Six rings glittered on her hands as she offered the bowl to Cal again. "Have some more?"

"Yes, thanks." He took a second serving. His appetite continued to amaze Libby. "I admire your work, Mrs. Stone."

"Really?" It still pleased her when anyone referred to her weaving as her "work." "Do you have a piece?"

"No, it's…out of my reach," he told her, remembering the display he'd seen behind glass at the Smithsonian.

"Where are you from, Hornblower?"

Cal switched his attention to Libby's father. "Philadelphia."

"Your work must involve a lot of traveling."

Cal didn't bother to suppress the grin. "More than you can imagine."

"Do you have a family?"

"My parents and my younger brother are still back… back east."

Despite himself, William thawed a bit. There had been something in Cal's eyes, in his voice, when he'd spoken of his family.

Enough, Libby decided, was enough. She pushed her bowl aside, picked up her tea with both hands, then leaned back, her eyes on her father. "If you have an application form handy, I'm sure Cal could fill it out. Then you'd have his date of birth and Social Security number, as well."

"A little snotty, aren't you?" Will commented over a forkful of salad.

"I'm snotty?"

"Don't apologize." Will patted her hand. "We are what we are. Tell me, Cal, what's your party affiliation?"

"Dad!"

"Just kidding." With a lopsided grin, he reached over to pull Libby onto his lap. "She was born here, you know."

"Yes, she told me." Cal watched Libby hook an arm around her father's neck.

"Used to play naked right out that door while I was gardening."

Despite herself, Libby laughed, even as she closed a hand over her father's throat. "Monster."

"Can I ask him what he thinks of Dylan?"

She gave his head a shake. "No."

"Bob Dylan or Dylan Thomas?" Cal asked, earning a narrowed look from William and one of surprise from Libby before she remembered his affection for poetry.

"Either," Will decided.

"Dylan Thomas was brilliant but depressing. I'd rather read Bob Dylan."

"Read?"

"The lyrics, Dad. Now that that's settled, why don't you tell me what you're doing here instead of driving your board of directors crazy?"

"I wanted to see my little girl."

She kissed him, just above the beard, because she

knew it was partially true. "I saw you when I got back from the South Pacific. Try again."

"And I wanted Caro to have the fresh air." He sent his wife a smug look over his daughter's shoulder. "We both figured the air around here worked well the first two times, so we'd try it again."

"What are you talking about?"

"I'm talking about this place being good for your mother's condition."

"Condition? You're sick?" Libby was up and grabbing her mother's hands. "What's wrong?"

"Will, you never could come to the point. What he's trying to say is I'm pregnant."

"Pregnant?" Libby felt her knees go weak. "But how?"

"And you call yourself a scientist," Cal murmured, and earned his first laugh from Will.

"But—" Too dazed to be annoyed by the comment, she looked back and forth between her parents. They were young, hardly more than forty, and vital. She knew there was nothing unusual about couples in their forties having babies. But they were her *parents*. "You're going to have a baby. I don't know what to say."

"Try congratulations," Will suggested.

"No. Yes, I mean. I need to sit down." She did, on the floor between their chairs. She discovered sitting wasn't enough and took three long breaths.

"How do you feel?" Caroline asked.

"Dazed." She looked up, studying her mother's face. "How do you feel?"

"Eighteen…though I have talked Will out of delivering this one himself here at the cabin, the way he did with you and Sunny."

"The woman's lost her sixties values," Will muttered, though he had been tremendously relieved when Caroline had insisted on an obstetrician and a hospital. "So what do you think, Libby?"

She rose to her knees so that she could hug each of them. "I think we should celebrate."

"I'm one step ahead of you." Rising, William went to the refrigerator, then held a bottle aloft. "Sparkling apple juice."

The cork popped with a sound as festive as champagne. They toasted each other, the baby, the absent Sunny, the past and the future. Cal joined them, drawn in by their pleasure in each other. Here was one more thing that time hadn't changed, he thought. The giddy delight a coming baby brought to people who wanted it.

He'd never thought very seriously about starting a family. He'd known that when the time, and the woman, were right the rest would fall into place. Now he caught himself imagining what it would be like if he and Libby were toasting their own expected child.

Dangerous thoughts. Impossible thoughts. He had

only a matter of days left with her—hours, really—and families required a lifetime.

Even as he yearned for one life, watching Libby's parents together reminded him of his own family. Were they watching the sky, wondering where he was, how he was? If only he could let them know he was safe.

"Cal?"

"Hmm? What?" He blinked and saw Libby staring at him. "I'm sorry."

"I was just saying we should build a fire."

"Sure."

"One of my favorite spots here is in front of the fire." Caroline hooked her arm through William's. "I'm so glad we stopped by for the night."

"For the night?" Libby repeated.

"We're on our way to Carmel," Caroline decided on the spot, and gave William's hand a vicious squeeze before he could speak. "I craved a ride along the Coast."

"What she craved was a cheeseburger under her alfalfa sprouts," William said. "That's when I knew she was pregnant."

"And being pregnant entitles me to an afternoon nap." Caroline sent her husband a slow smile. "Why don't you tuck me in?"

"I could use a nap myself." With his arm around her shoulders, they started out. "Carmel? Last I heard we were spending a week here. Since when are we going to Carmel?"

"Since four's a crowd, dummy."

"That may be, but I haven't decided if I like the idea of Libby being with him."

"She likes it." Caroline walked into the bedroom and was flooded with memories. The nights they'd shared, and the mornings. They'd made love in that bed, argued politics, planned ways to save the world from itself. She'd laughed there, cried there and given birth there. She sat on the edge and let her hands run over the spread. She could almost feel the murmur of memories.

Will, his hands tucked in the back pockets of his jeans, paced to the window.

She smiled at his back, remembering how he had been at eighteen. Even thinner, she recalled, even more idealistic, and just as wonderful. They had always loved this place, being children there, having children there. Even when things had changed, they had never lost that cocksure certainty of who and what they were. She understood him, heard his thoughts as if they were in her own head.

"A cargo pilot," Will muttered. "And what the hell kind of name is Hornblower? There's something about him, Caro, I don't know what, but something I'm not sure rings true."

"Don't you trust Liberty?"

"Of course I do." He looked back, insulted. "It's him I don't trust."

"Ah, the echo of time." She cupped a hand to her ear. "The exact words my father once spoke when referring to you."

"He was a poor judge of character," Will muttered, and turned back to the window.

"Most men are when it comes to the choices their daughters make. I remember you telling my father that I knew my own mind. Let's see, was that the first or second time he threw you out of the house?"

"Both." He had to grin. "He said you'd be back in six months and that I'd end up selling daisies on a street corner. Fooled him, didn't we?"

"That was nearly twenty-five years ago."

"Don't rub it in." He fingered his beard. "Doesn't it bother you that they're here—together?"

"You mean that they're lovers?"

"Yes." He dug his hands in his pockets again. "She's our baby."

"I remember you telling me once that making love was the most natural expression of trust and affection between two people. That hang-ups about sex needed to be eradicated if the world was ever to experience true peace and goodwill."

"I did not."

"You certainly did. We were crammed into the back seat of your VW, steaming up the windows, at the time."

He had to grin. "It must have worked."

"It did, mostly because I'd already decided you were the one I wanted. You were the first man I'd ever loved, Will, so I knew it was right." She held out a hand and waited until he'd clasped it. "That man downstairs is the first Libby's ever loved. She knows what's right." He started to object, but she tightened her grip. "We raised them to follow their hearts. Did we make a mistake?"

"No." He laid a palm on the gentle slope of her belly. "We'll do the same for this one."

"He has kind eyes," she said softly. "When he looks at her, his heart's in them."

"You always were overly romantic. That's how I caught you."

"And kept me," she murmured against his lips.

"Right." He toyed with the hem of her sweater, knowing how easy it would be to slip it over her head, and exactly what he would find beneath. "You don't really want to sleep, do you?"

With a laugh, she overbalanced so that they both tumbled onto the bed.

"It's so strange." Libby dropped down on the grass beside the stream. "Thinking that my parents are going to have another child. They looked happy, didn't they?"

"Very." Cal settled beside her. "Except when your father was scowling at me."

She laughed a little as she rested her head on his shoulder. "Sorry. He's really a very friendly man, most of the time."

"I'll take your word for it." He plucked at a blade of grass. It hardly mattered if he had her father's approval or not. Soon Cal would be out of his life, and out of Libby's.

She loved it here beside the water, which ran fresh and cold over the rocks. The grass was long and soft, dotted along the bank with small blue flowers. There would be foxglove in the summer, growing as tall as a man and bending over the stream with its purple or white bells. There would be lilies and columbine. At dusk deer would come to drink, and sometimes a lumbering bear would come fishing.

She didn't want to think of summer, but of now, when the air was as fresh as the water, with a clear, clean taste to it. Chipmunks raced in the forest beyond. She and Sunny had hand-fed the friendlier ones.

Wherever she went, to remote islands, to desert outposts, she would remember those early years of her life. And be grateful for them.

"That's going to be a very lucky baby," she murmured. Then she smiled as a thought struck her. "To think, after all these years, I might have a brother."

He thought of his own, Jacob, with his flaring temper and his sharp, impatient mind. "I always wanted a sister."

"There's something to be said for them, too. But they always seem to be prettier than you are."

He rolled her onto the grass. "I wish I could meet your Sunbeam. Ow." He rubbed a hand over his side where she'd pinched him.

"Concentrate on me."

"That's all I seem to do." He braced his arm beside her head as he studied her face. "I have to go back to the ship for a little while."

She tried valiantly to keep the sorrow out of her eyes. It had been easy to pretend there was no ship, and no tomorrow. "I didn't have a chance to ask you how it was going."

Quickly, he thought. Too quickly. "I'll know more when I check the computer. Can you make an excuse to your parents if I'm not back when they get up?"

"I'll tell them you're off meditating. My father will love it."

"Okay. Then tonight…" He lowered his head for a gentle kiss. "I'll concentrate on you."

"Concentrating's all you'll do." She linked her arms around his neck. "You're sleeping on the couch."

"I am?"

"Definitely."

"In that case…" He slid down to her.

* * *

Later, during the night, when the fire was burning low and the house was quiet, Cal sat alone, fully dressed. He knew how to get back. At least he knew how he had gotten where and when he was and how to reverse the process.

With a few more repairs, basically unnecessary ones, he would be ready to go. Technically he would be ready. But emotionally... Nothing had ever torn him quite so neatly in two.

If she asked him to stay... God, he was afraid if she did, it would swing the balance of the tug-of-war he was waging. But she wouldn't ask him to stay. He couldn't ask her to go.

Perhaps when he made it back and offered the data to the world of science a new, less dangerous way would be created to conquer time. Perhaps he could come back.

Turning his head, he looked into the fire. More fantasies. Libby was facing the facts, and so would he.

He thought he heard her on the stairs. But when he looked it was William.

"Trouble sleeping?" he asked Cal.

"Some. You?"

"I always loved this place at night." Because he loved his daughter, as well, he was determined to make an effort to be civil, if not exactly friendly. "The quiet, the dark." He stooped to add another log to the fire. Sparks flew, then winked out. "I never pictured myself living anywhere else."

"I never imagined living in a place like this or realized how hard it would be to leave."

"A long way from Philadelphia."

"A very long way."

He recognized gloom when he heard it. William had courted it early in his youth, mistaking it for romance. Unbending a little, he dug out the brandy and two snifters. "Want a drink?"

"Yeah. Thanks."

William settled in the winged chair and stretched out his long legs. "I used to sit here at night and ponder the meaning of life."

"Did you ever figure it out?"

"Sometimes I did, sometimes I didn't."

It had been simpler, somehow, when his main concerns had been world peace and social reform. Now, God help him, he was nearing middle age—that area that had always seemed so gray and distant. It reminded him that he had once been a young man, much younger than the one facing him now, with his head in the clouds and his mind on a woman. The times they are a-changing, he thought wryly, and swirled his brandy.

"Are you in love with Libby?"

"I was just asking myself that same question."

William sipped his brandy. He preferred the traces of doubt and frustration he heard to a glib response. He'd always been glib. No wonder Caroline's father had detested him. "Come up with an answer?"

"Not a comfortable one."

Nodding, William lifted his glass. "Before I met Caro, I was planning to join the Peace Corps or a Tibetan monastery. She was fresh out of high school. Her father wanted to shoot me."

Cal grinned. He was beginning to enjoy the brandy. "I had a minute to be grateful you didn't have a weapon this afternoon."

"Being a pacifist by nature, I only gave it a passing thought," William assured him. "Caro's father thrived on the idea. I can't wait to tell him I got her pregnant again." Relaxed now, he savored the idea.

"Libby's hoping for a brother."

"Did she say that?" Now he grinned, lingering over the idea of a son. "She was my first. Every child's a miracle, but the first…I guess you never get over it."

"She is a miracle. She changed my life."

William's look sharpened. Hornblower might not realize he was in love, he thought, but there was little doubt about it. "Caro likes you," he commented. "She has a way of seeing into the heart of people. I only want to say that Libby isn't as sturdy as she seems. Be careful with her."

He rose then, afraid he might start to pontificate. "Get some sleep," he advised. "Caro's bound to be up at dawn fixing whole-wheat pancakes or yogurt-and-kiwi surprise." He winced a little. He was a man who would always yearn in his heart for bacon and eggs. "You won points by the way you dug into that tofu amandine casserole."

"It was great."

"No wonder she likes you." He paused at the foot of the steps. "You know, I have a sweater just like that."

"Really?" Cal couldn't suppress the grin. "Small world."

Chapter 10

"I knew you'd be up early." Libby slipped out the back door to join her mother.

"Not so early." Caroline sighed, annoyed with herself for missing the sunrise. "I've found myself getting a slower start the last couple of months."

"Morning sickness?"

"No." Smiling, Caroline hooked an arm around Libby's waist. "It seems all three of my children decided to spare me that. Did I ever tell you I appreciated it?"

"No."

"Well, I do." She gave Libby's cheek a quick kiss and noted the faint shadows under her eyes. Biding her time, she nodded toward the trees. "Like to walk?"

"Yes, I would."

They started off at a meandering pace, the bells Caroline wore at her wrists and ears jingling cheerfully. So much was the same, Libby thought. The trees, the sky, the quiet cabin behind them. And so much had changed. She leaned her head against her mother's shoulder for a moment.

"Do you remember when we used to walk like this, you and Sunny and I?"

"I remember walking with you." Caroline laughed as the branches arched overhead in a cool, green tunnel. "Sunny never walked anywhere. The moment she could stand she was off at a dash. You and I would poke along, just as we're doing now."

And what would this child be like? Caroline wondered, feeling a fresh thrill of anticipation.

"Then we'd pick some flowers or berries so that Dad would think we'd been doing something productive."

"It seems both our men are sleeping in today." When Libby didn't respond, Caroline waited until the silence between them was comfortable again. The forest was alive with sounds, the rustling of small game in the brush, the call of birds in flight. "I like your friend, Libby."

"I'm glad you do. I wanted you to." She bent to pick up a twig, then broke small pieces off as she walked. It was a nervous gesture Caroline knew very well. Sunny would let any and all feeling burst straight out, but Libby, her quiet, sensible Libby, would hold them in.

"It's more important that you do."

"I do, very much." Suddenly aware of what she was doing, Libby tossed the rest of the twig aside. "He's kind and funny and strong. This time I've had here with him, it's been wonderful for me. I never really thought I'd find someone who would make me feel the way Caleb makes me feel."

"But you don't smile when you say that." Caroline reached up to touch her daughter's face. "Why?"

"This…time we have…it's only temporary."

"I don't understand. Why temporary? If you're in love with him—"

"I am," Libby murmured. "Very much in love with him."

"Then?"

Libby drew a long breath. It was impossible to explain, she thought. "He has to go back, to his family."

"To Philadelphia?" Caroline prompted her, at a loss.

"Yes…" There was a smile now, faint and wistful. "To Philadelphia."

"I don't see why that should make a difference," she began. Then stopped and put a hand on Libby's arm. "Oh, baby, is he married?"

"No." She might have laughed then, but she noted the deep and genuine concern in her mother's eyes. "No, it's nothing like that. Caleb could never be dishonest. It's very hard to explain, but I can tell you that right from the start we both knew that Cal would have to go back where he belonged, and I...I would have to stay."

"A few thousand miles shouldn't matter if two people want to be together."

"Sometimes distance is, well, longer than it looks. Don't worry." Leaning over, she kissed Caroline's cheek. "I can honestly say that I wouldn't trade the time I've had with Cal for anything. There was a poster in the cabin when I was little. Do you remember? It said something about...if you had something, let it go. If it didn't come back to you, it was never yours."

"I never liked that poster," Caroline muttered.

This time Libby did laugh. "Let's pick some flowers."

Libby watched them go a few hours later, her father behind the wheel of the rumbling pickup, her mother's earrings dancing as she leaned out of the window to wave until she was out of sight.

"I like your parents."

Libby turned to Cal, linking her hands around his neck. "They liked you, too."

He leaned down for a brief kiss. "Your mother, maybe."

"My father, too."

"If I had a year or two to win him over he might almost like me."

"He wasn't scowling at you today."

"No." He rubbed his cheek against hers as he considered. "It was down to a sneer. What are you going to tell them?"

"About what?"

"About why I'm not here, with you?"

"I'll tell them that you went home." Because she made the effort, her answer sounded casual and easy. So easy that he nearly swore.

"Just like that?"

Her voice was a little brittle now, she knew, with a tone that could easily be taken as callous. "They won't pry if I don't want them to. It will be simpler for everyone if I tell them the truth."

"Which is?"

Was he determined to make it difficult? She moved her shoulders restlessly. "Things didn't work out, and you went on with your life. I went on with mine."

"Yeah, I guess that's best. No mess, no regrets."

Irritable, she thrust her fists in her pockets. "You have a better idea?"

"No. Yours is just dandy." He pulled away, annoyed with himself, annoyed with her. "I've got to get to the ship."

"I know. I thought I'd run into town and pick up

the camera and some other things. If I get back early enough I'll ride out, check on your progress."

"Fine." He was damned if it was going to be so easy for her when he was being torn in two. Before he could regret it, he yanked her against him and crushed his mouth down on hers.

Hot, edgy, tasting of anger and frustration, the kiss spun out. Libby hung on, to maintain her physical, as well as her emotional, balance. She couldn't, wouldn't, give him what he seemed to need. Total capitulation. He'd never asked for that before, nor had she known she would so firmly withhold it. Trapped, she couldn't soothe, couldn't demand, as he devoured.

In one long, possessive stroke, his hands ran up her body, then down again with no lessening of force. She might have protested. There was something here that frightened her, that left her weak—not meltingly, but with an open-ended vulnerability that made her struggle to find her feet again. There was no gentleness here, nor was there the sense of urgent desire he had once shown her. Instead, the kiss was like a punishment, and a brutally effective one.

"Caleb—" she began, hitching in a shallow breath, when he released her.

"That should give you something to think about," he said, then turned abruptly to stalk away.

Stunned, she stared after him. One unsteady hand

reached up to press against lips still tender from his assault. When her breathing steadied, her temper took hold. She'd think about it, all right. She stormed inside, slamming the door behind her. Moments later she stormed out again to climb into the Land Rover.

It was all going perfectly. And he was mad as hell. Technically he could take off within twenty-four hours. The major repairs were done, the calculations as finely tuned as he and the computer could make them in the time allotted. His ship was ready. He wasn't. That was what it came down to.

She was certainly ready to see him off, Cal thought as he fused a tear in the inner shell with his spot laser. Damned anxious, if it came to that. She was probably in town right now buying a camera so that she could take a few souvenir pictures before she waved goodbye. He shut off the laser and checked the seam.

Why did she have to be so practical about it?

Because she was practical, he reminded himself as he yanked off his protective goggles. That was one of the things he most admired about her. She was practical, warm, intelligent, shy. He could still see the way her eyes had looked the first time he'd told her he wanted her. They'd gone from big and tawny to big and confused.

And when he'd touched her. She'd gotten hot and

trembly. She was soft, so incredibly soft. Cursing himself, he stowed the laser in the tool compartment, then tossed the goggles in beside them before he slammed the door. He couldn't imagine a man in the universe being able to resist those eyes, or that skin, or that wide, sexy mouth.

That was part of the problem, he admitted as he prowled the ship. Men wouldn't. Maybe she hadn't paid attention before. Maybe she'd been too wrapped up in her books and her work and her theories on the societal tendencies of man as a species. One day she was going to slip those glasses off her nose and look around—and realize that there were men, flesh-and-blood men, looking back at her. Men who could make promises, he thought in disgust. Even if they didn't mean to keep them.

Perhaps she hadn't realized how much passion, how much heat, how much power, she held. But he'd opened those doors for her. Opened, hell—he'd smashed them. Once he was gone, other men would tend the fire he'd lit.

The thought made him insane. Cal admitted it as he dragged his hands through his hair. Stark, raving crazy. He belonged in one of those padded cells Libby had spoken of. He couldn't stand it—the thought of someone else touching her, kissing her. Undressing her.

With an oath, he wheeled into his cabin and began to put it in order. That is, he tossed things around.

He was being selfish and unfair. And he didn't care. It was true that he would have to accept the fact that Libby would go on with her life, and that her life would include a lover—or lovers, he thought, grinding his teeth. A husband, perhaps, and children. He had to accept that. But he was damned if he had to like it.

After kicking a shoe into a corner, he dug his hands into his pockets and stared at the picture of his family. His parents, he mused, going over each feature of their faces as he had never bothered to before. It had been three...no, four months since he'd seen them. If you didn't count the centuries.

They were attractive, strong-looking people, despite his father's slightly hangdog expression. They had always seemed so content to him, so sure of their lives and what they wanted. He liked to picture them at home, with his mother laboring over some thick technical book and his father whistling between his teeth as he played with his flowers.

He had his mother's nose. Intrigued, Cal leaned down to peer closer. Strange, he'd never noticed that before. Apparently she'd been satisfied with the one she'd been born with and had passed it on to him.

And to Jacob, he realized as he studied his brother's image. But to Jacob she'd passed along brilliance, as well. Brilliance wasn't always a gift, Caleb thought with a grin. It seemed to make Jacob hotheaded, questioning and impatient. He remembered his mother saying that J.T., as his family called him, was more fond of arguing than breathing.

Cal decided he'd probably inherited his father's more even temperament. Except he didn't feel very even-tempered at the moment.

With a sigh, he sat on the bed. "You'd like her," he murmured to the images. "I wish you could meet her." That was a first, he thought. He'd never had the urge to bring any of his companions home for family approval. It was probably the result of spending the day with Libby's parents.

He was stalling. Rubbing his hands over his face, Cal admitted he was wasting his time with busywork and self-indulgent analysis. He should already be gone. But he'd promised himself another day. There was Libby's time capsule to do…that is, if she was still speaking to him.

She was bound to be angry about the little number he'd pulled on her before he'd left that morning. That was fine, he decided as he stretched out. He'd rather have her angry than smilingly urging him on his way. Lazily he checked his watch. She should be back in a couple hours.

Right now he was going to have a nap to make up

for the long, frustrating and sleepless night he'd spent on her couch. Switching on the sleep tape beside the bed, he closed his eyes and tuned out.

Idiot, Libby thought, gripping the wheel tightly as she maneuvered the Land Rover along the winding switchback toward home. Conceited idiot, she clarified. He'd better have an explanation when she saw him again. No matter how she racked her brain, she could come up with no reason why he had kissed her in that furious, mean-spirited way.

Something to think about.

Well, she had thought about it, Libby reminded herself while she navigated the narrowing dirt road. It still made her furious. And it still didn't make any sense. Then again, she had a twice-married neighbor in Portland who claimed men never made sense.

They always had to her—as a species, anyway, Libby thought grimly. And on paper. Now, for the first time, she was involved in a one-on-one with a flesh-and-blood member of the male genus, and she was baffled.

Libby bumped over rocks as she tried once again to solve the mystery of Caleb Hornblower.

Perhaps it had had something to do with the visit by her parents. But then, he'd been moody the morning before they had arrived. Moody, but not angry, she remembered, and they had made slow, quiet love by the stream during the afternoon. He'd seemed cheerful enough at dinner, perhaps a little withdrawn, but that was only natural. It must be very difficult for him to be around people when he had to concentrate on not saying anything that might give him away.

She felt a tug of sympathy and stubbornly ignored it.

That was no reason for him to take his frustration out on her. Wasn't she trying to help him? It was killing her inside, but she was doing everything in her power to see that he got back to where he wanted to be.

She had her own life, as well. That fact soothed only a little as she barreled up a slope. She should be working on her dissertation and making the preliminary plans for her next field study. There was an offer of a lecture tour she had yet to fully consider. Instead, she was running errands—buying cameras and oatmeal cookies. For the last time, she decided huffily, but then she realized that it would indeed be the last time.

She stopped the Land Rover when the trail narrowed to a footpath. She hadn't really meant to come out to Caleb. During the entire trip she'd told herself she would go back to the cabin and get to work. Yet here she was, letting herself be pulled back. At least there was something she could do for herself.

On impulse, she grabbed the new Polaroid from the shopping bag. After unboxing it, she skimmed over the directions, then loaded it with the first of the packs of film she'd bought. As an afterthought, she grabbed the bag of chunky oatmeal cookies.

From the top of the slope she studied the ship. It lay huge and silent on the rocks and the downed trees, like some strange sleeping animal. Deliberately she blocked out thoughts of the man inside and concentrated on the ship itself.

The sixteen-wheeler of the future, she decided, carefully framing it. The Greyhound bus or power van. All aboard for Mars, Mercury and Venus. Express trips to Pluto and Orion available. With what was more a sigh than a snicker, she took two pictures. Sitting on the edge of the slope, she watched them develop. Fifty years ago, she mused, the idea of instant pictures had been science fiction. She glanced back at the ship. Man worked fast. Very fast.

Wanting a few more moments to herself, she ripped open the bag of cookies and began to nibble.

Of course, she'd never be able to show the picture that was already taking shape in her hand to anyone. One was for the capsule, but the other was for her personal files. She wanted to believe it was the scientist who had taken it, who would label and file it along with other pictures she would take and the hard copy of the report she was writing on this isolated experience.

But it had nothing to do with science, and everything to do with the heart. She didn't want to rely on her memory.

She slipped the pictures into her pocket, swung the camera over her shoulder and started down.

When she reached the hatch, she lifted her fist, then started to laugh. Did one knock on the door of a spacecraft? Feeling foolish with the ship looming over her, she rapped twice. A chipmunk scurried over the ground, scrambled onto the trunk of a fallen tree and stared at her.

"I know it's odd," Libby told him. "Just remember to keep it under your hat." She tossed half a cookie in his direction, then turned back to knock again. "All right, Hornblower, open up. I feel like an idiot out here."

She tried knocking, pounding, shouting. Once she gave in to temper and slammed the hull with a good kick. Favoring her sore toes, she stepped back. Furious with him, she'd nearly decided to turn back when it occurred to her he might not be able to hear her.

Stepping closer, she began to search for the device he had used to open the hatch. It took her ten minutes. When the hatch opened, she stormed inside, ready for a fight.

"Listen, Hornblower, I—"

He wasn't on the bridge. Frustrated, Libby dragged back her hair. Couldn't he even make himself available when she wanted to yell at him?

The shield was up. She hadn't been able to see in from the outside, but now she had a stunning panoramic view. Drawn, she crossed over to the controls. How would it feel, she wondered as she sat in his chair, to pilot something so huge, so powerful? She scanned the buttons and switches spread out before her. Was it any wonder he loved it? Even a woman who had always been firmly rooted to the ground could imagine the wild, limitless freedom of traveling through space. There would be planets, balls of color and light. The glimmer of distant stars, the glow of orbiting moons.

She liked to think of him that way, weaving through the stars the way he had woven through the trees with her on the cycle.

Libby took a last scan of the controls, then studied the computer. A little ill at ease, she glanced around the empty bridge before she leaned forward.

"Computer?"

Working.

She jolted, then swallowed a nervous laugh. There were two questions she wanted to ask, but only one she truly wanted the answer to. Because she believed in facing facts, Libby inhaled, exhaled, then plunged.

"Computer, what is the status on the calculations for the return journey to the twenty-third century?"

Calculations complete. Probability index formulated.

*Risk factors, trajectory, thrust, degree of orbit, veloc-
ity and success factors locked in. Is report desired?*

"No."

So he was finished. She'd known it, even when she'd
tried to tell herself she had a few more days with him.
He hadn't told her, but she thought she understood why.
Cal wouldn't want to hurt her, and he would know,
would have to know, how she felt. No matter how hard
she tried to treat their relationship as a single moment
in time, one based on passion and affection and mutual need, he had seen through her. He was trying to
be kind.

She wanted to be glad for him. She had to be glad
for him.

She took a minute to adjust, then asked what she had
asked once before.

"Computer."

Working.

"Who is Caleb Hornblower?"

*Hornblower, Caleb, Captain ISF, retired. Born 2
February, to Katrina Hardesty Hornblower and Byram
Edward Hornblower. Place of birth Philadelphia, Penn-
sylvania. Graduate Wilson Freemont Memorial Acad-
emy. Attended Princeton University, withdrew after
sixteen months without degree. Enlisted ISF. Served
six years, seven months. Military record as follows...*

With her lips pursed, Libby listened to the readout of

Cal's military career. There was citation after citation— just as there was reprimand after reprimand. His record as a pilot was flawless. His disciplinary record was an entirely different matter. She couldn't help but smile.

She thought of her father and his ingrained distrust of the military system. Yes, given a bit of time, she thought, he would have grown very fond of Cal.

Credit rating 5.8, the computer continued.

"Stop." Libby heaved a sigh. She wasn't interested in Cal's credit rating. She'd pried far enough into his personal life as it was. Any other answers she wanted would have to come from him. And quickly.

Rising, she began to wander through the ship, looking for him.

It was the music that tipped her off. She heard it first, distant and lovely, with a vague curiosity. Something classical, with a kind of swelling passion. As she followed it, she tried to identify the composer.

She found Cal asleep in his cabin. The music filled the room, every corner of it, yet it was soft, soothing, seductive. She felt the tug, the almost irresistible urge to slip into the bed beside him, snuggling close until he woke and made slow, sweet love to her.

She shook it off. The music, she decided. Somehow it was comforting and erotic at the same time. Exactly the way his kisses could be. She wouldn't let it influence her or let herself forget that she was angry with him.

Still, she took a picture of him as he slept, then slipped it, almost guiltily, into her pocket.

After leaning against the doorway, she lifted her chin. It was a deliberately defiant pose, and she enjoyed it.

"So this is how you work."

Though she'd pitched her voice above the music, he went on sleeping. She considered going over and giving his shoulder a shove, then came up with a better idea. She slipped two fingers of her left hand into her mouth, inhaled, then blew out a sharp, shrill whistle, just as Sunny had taught her.

He came up in the bed like a rocket. "Red alert!" he shouted before he saw her smirking at him from the doorway. After leaning back against the cushioned headboard, he ran a hand over his eyes.

He'd been dreaming. Out in space, whipping through the galaxy, with the controls at his fingertips and worlds racing by hundreds of thousands of miles beneath him. She'd been there, right beside him, an arm wrapped around his waist, all the fascination, all the thrill of flying glowing on her face.

Until something had gone wrong. And the ship had shaken, the gauges had blinked, the bells had sounded. He'd heard her scream as they'd gone into a dive. He hadn't known what to do. Quite suddenly his mind had gone blank. He hadn't been able to save her.

Here she was now, while his heart was still sprinting from the dream, looking cocky and ready to spar.

"What the hell was that for?"

He looked as though he'd had a scare. She certainly hoped so. "It seemed the most efficient way to wake you up. I tell you, Hornblower, you keep working like this, you'll wear yourself right out."

"I was taking a break." He wished he'd taken a good long slug of potent, electric-blue Antellis liquor. "I didn't sleep much last night."

"Too bad." As sympathy went, it left a lot to be desired. Still studying him, she dug for a cookie.

"That couch is lumpy."

"I'll make a note of it. Maybe that's why you woke up on the wrong side of it." She took her time, nipping off tiny bite after tiny bite. It was an attempt to make him hungry, and she succeeded, though not in the way she'd intended.

He could feel his muscles tightening, each separate one. "I don't know what you mean."

"It's an expression."

"I've heard it." He knew he snapped the words out, but he couldn't help it. She flicked out her tongue to catch a crumb at the corner of her mouth. He nearly groaned. "I didn't wake up on the wrong side of anything."

"Well, I suppose it could be your nature to be surly and you've managed to repress it lately."

"I'm not surly." He all but growled it.

"No? Arrogant, then. Is that better?" Her slow half smile was meant to annoy, but it provoked a different emotion.

Trying to ignore her and what was going on inside his own rebellious body, he looked at his watch. "You took a long time in town."

"My time's my own, Hornblower."

His brows arched. If she hadn't been so smug about her own control, she might have noticed that the eyes beneath them had darkened. "You want to fight?"

"Me?" Her lips turned up again. She was the very picture of innocence. "Why, Caleb, after meeting my parents you should know I'm a born pacifist. I was rocked to sleep with folk songs."

He muttered an opinion, a single two-syllable word that Libby had always thought belonged to the slang of the twentieth century. Intrigued, she cocked her head.

"So, that's still the response when someone doesn't have a clever or intelligent answer. It's such a comfort to know some traditions survive."

He threw his legs off the edge of the bed and, his eyes on hers, slowly unfolded himself. He didn't step toward her, not yet. Not until he could trust himself not to plant a good clean jab on her outthrust chin. Strange, he'd never noticed the stubborn set of it before. Or that I-dare-you look in her eyes.

The worst of it was, the arrogance was every bit as arousing as the warmth.

"You're pushing, babe. I figure it's only fair to warn you that I don't come from a particularly peaceful family."

"Well…" Carefully she chose another cookie. "That certainly puts the fear of God into me." After rolling up the bag, she tossed it at him so that his defensive catch crumbled half the contents. "I don't know what's gotten under your skin, Hornblower, but I've got better things to do than worry about it. You can stay here and sulk if you like, but I'm going back to work."

She barely managed to turn around. He grabbed her arms and had her pressed into the wall, his fingers digging in. Later she would wonder why she had been surprised that he could move that quickly, or that beneath the easy disposition there lurked a fierce, raw-edged temper.

"You want to know what's wrong with me?" His eyes, so close to hers, were the color that edged lightning bolts. "Is that what all this button-pushing's about, Libby?"

"I don't care what's wrong with you." She kept her chin up, though her mouth had gone dry. Libby knew that for her offering an apology would always be easier than sticking with a fight. Sometimes it wasn't pacifism but cowardice. She straightened her spine and drew in a deep breath. She was sticking.

"I don't give a damn what's wrong with you. Now let me go."

"You should." He wrapped her hair around his hand to pull her head back, slowly exposing her throat. "Do you think that every emotion a man has toward a woman is gentle, kind, loving?"

"I'm not a fool." She began to struggle, and she was more annoyed than afraid when he didn't release her.

"No, you're not." Her eyes were on his, fury matching fury. He thought he felt something break inside him, the last bolt that had caged the uncivilized. "Maybe it's time I taught you the rest."

"I don't need you to teach me anything."

"That's right, there'll be others to teach you, won't there?" Jealousy clawed deep, drawing thick, hot blood. "Damn you. And damn them, every one of them. Think of this. Whenever anyone else touches you, tomorrow, ten years from tomorrow, you'll wish it was me. I'll see to it."

With his words still hanging in the air, he pulled her to the bed.

Chapter 11

She fought him. She refused to be taken in anger, no matter how deep her love. The bed sank beneath their combined weights, molding to them like a cocoon. The music drifted, calm and beautiful. His hands were rough as they dragged at the buttons of her shirt.

She didn't speak. It never occurred to her to beg him to stop, or to give in to the tears that would surely have snapped him back to his senses. Instead she struggled, trying to roll away from his ruthlessly seeking hands. She fought, furiously bucking, pushing against him, waging a private war against the traitorous response of her body, which would betray her heart.

She would hate him for this. The knowledge nearly broke her. If he succeeded in what he set out to do, it would wash away other memories and leave this one, this violent, distorted one, dominant. Unable to bear it, she fought now for both of them.

He knew her too well. Every curve, every dip, every pulse. On a wave of fury, he locked her wrists in one hand and dragged her arms over her head. His mouth savaged her neck while his free hand slid down, unerringly, to find one of those secret, vulnerable places. He heard her moan as the unwanted, unavoidable pleasure tore into her. Her body tensed, a wire ready to snap. It arched, a bow pulled taut. He felt the burst of release as it shuddered through her, heard her choked-off cry. He saw her lips quiver before she pressed them hard together.

Regret burned through him. He had no right, no one did, to take something beautiful and use it as a weapon. He'd wanted to hurt her for something beyond her control. And he had. No more, he realized, than he had hurt himself.

"Libby."

She only shook her head, her eyes tightly closed. Wishing for words that weren't there, Cal rolled over and stared at the ceiling.

"I have no excuse...there is no excuse for treating you that way."

She managed to swallow the tears. It relieved her, made it possible for her to steady her breathing and open her eyes. "Maybe not, but there's usually a reason. I'd like to hear it."

He didn't answer for a long time. They lay close and tense, not quite touching. There were dozens of reasons he could give her—lack of sleep, overwork, the anxiety over the possible failure of his flight. They would all be accurate, to a point. But they wouldn't be the truth. Libby, he knew, set great store by honesty.

"I care for you," he said slowly. "It isn't easy knowing I won't see you again. I realize we both have our own lives," he added before she could speak. "Our own place. Maybe we're both doing what has to be done, but I don't like the idea that it's easy for you."

"It isn't."

He knew it was selfish, but it relieved him to hear it. Reaching over, he linked his hand with hers. "I'm jealous."

"Of what?"

"Of the men you'll meet, the ones you'll love. The one's who'll love you."

"But—"

"No, don't say anything. Let me get it all out and over with. It doesn't seem to matter that I know it's wrong, intellectually. It's a gut reaction, Libby, and I'm used to going with them. Every time I imagine another man touching you the way I've touched you, seeing you the way I've seen you, I go a little crazy."

"And that's why you've been angry with me?" She turned her head to study his profile. "Over my imagined future affairs?"

"I guess you've got a right to make me sound like an idiot."

"I'm not trying to."

He moved his shoulders in what might have been a shrug. "I can even see him. He's about six-four and built like one of those Greek gods."

"Adonis," she suggested, smiling. "He gets my vote."

"Shut up." But she noted that his lips curved slightly. "He's got blond hair, streaked, kind of windswept, and this strong, rock-hard jaw with one of those clefts in it."

"Like Kirk Douglas?"

He shot her a suspicious look. "You know a guy like this?"

"Only by reputation." Because she sensed that the storm was over, she kissed Cal's shoulder.

"Anyway, he's got brains, too, which is another reason I really hate him. He's a doctor, not medical but philosophy. He can discuss the traditional mating habits of obscure tribes with you for hours. And he plays piano."

"Wow. I'm impressed."

"He's rich," Cal went on, almost viciously. "A 9.2 credit rating. He takes you to Paris and makes love to you in a room overlooking the Seine. Then he gives you a diamond as big as a fist."

"Well, well." She gave it some thought. "Can he quote poetry?"

"He even writes it."

"Oh, my God." She put a hand to her heart. "I don't suppose you could tell me where I'm going to meet him? I want to be ready."

He rolled over just enough to look at her. Her eyes were bright, but with amusement, not tears. "You're getting a real charge out of this, aren't you?"

"Yes." She lifted a hand to his face. "I suppose it might make you feel better if I promised I'd join a convent."

"Okay." He took her wrist to bring her palm against his mouth. "Can I get it in writing?"

"I'll think about it." His eyes were clear again, deep and clear. He was Cal now, the man she could love and understand. "Are we finished fighting?"

"Looks like it. I'm sorry, Libby. I've been acting like a lupz."

"I'm not sure what that means, but you're probably right."

"Friends?" He bent down to brush her lips with his.

"Friends." Before he could draw back, she cupped his head in her hand and held him against her for a longer, deeper and much less friendly kiss. "Cal?"

"Hmm?" He traced her lips with his tongue, memorizing their shape and texture.

"Did this guy have a name? Ouch!" Torn between laughter and pain, she jerked back. "You bit me."

"Damn right."

"It was your fantasy," she reminded him primly, "not mine."

"And let's keep it that way." But he was grinning as he ran his hand up the smooth skin where her shirt had parted. "I can give you others, if you're willing to settle."

"Yes." His palm rounded over her breast, working magic. "Oh, yes."

"If I took you to Paris, we'd spend the first three days in that hotel suite and never get out of bed." He continued to tease, nipping here, stroking there, stopping just short of possession. "We'd drink champagne, bottle after bottle, and eat small dishes with exotic names and tastes. I'd know every inch of your body, every pore of your skin. We'd stay in that big, soft bed and go places no one else had ever been."

"Cal." She trembled as he circled her breasts with slow, openmouthed kisses.

"Then we'd get dressed. I can see you in something thin and white, something that skims off your shoulders, dips down your back. Something that makes every man who sees you want to murder me."

"I don't even see them." With a sigh, she traced her

hands down him, lingering over every plane and angle. "I only see you."

"The stars are out. Millions of them. You can smell Paris. It's rich...water and flowers. We'd walk for miles so you could see all those incredible lights and wonderful ancient buildings. We'd stop and drink wine in a café at a table with an umbrella. Then we'd go back and make love again, for hours and hours."

His lips came back to hers, drugging her. "We don't need Paris for that."

"No." He braced himself over her, bracketing her head between his hands. Her face was already glowing, her eyes were half closed, that soft smile was on her lips. He wanted to remember this, this one instant when there was nothing and no one but her.

"Oh, God, Libby, I need you."

It was all she needed to hear, all she would ever ask to hear. She reached up to enfold him.

There was urgency here. She could taste it as his tongue plunged deep into her mouth, demanding. Impatient, his hands molded her body. Because his feelings mirrored her own, her response was explosive. Her blood was molten, throbbing as it flowed close under her skin. The heat was unbearable. Delicious. It grew only more intense as he stripped her.

A primitive sound hummed deep in her throat. With a speed and fury that rocked him, she was yanking off his shirt, dragging his jeans over his hips. Desperate, she rolled, reversing their positions, making a fast, hot journey over him. She heard his breath catch, and the sound sent her excitement soaring to new heights.

Power. It was indeed the ultimate aphrodisiac. She could make him tremble and ache and whisper her name. She'd never known that with such little effort she could make him helpless.

And he was beautiful. The feel of him under her hands, the taste of him that lingered on her tongue. And strong. There were ridges of muscles, firm, tight. But they trembled under the delicate dance of her fingertips.

He'd wanted to make her remember. Cal groaned under the weight of the sensations she was bringing to him. It was he who would remember, always. The music that he had always loved, the simple eloquence of it, filled his head. He knew it would remind him of her from now to forever.

He could feel the heat radiate from her as she moved her body up his, searching, finding his mouth. Her kiss was slow, sultry, something he could drown in. Then she was laughing, evading his questing hands as she drove him toward madness again.

He couldn't bear it. His heart was pounding against his ribs, echoed by dozens of frantic pulses throughout his body. The rhythm seemed to call out her name, again and again, until he was filled with it.

"Libby." The word was hoarse, as raw as his need. "For God's sake."

Then she closed over him like hot velvet. The sound she made was hardly more than a moan, but it vibrated with triumph. Lost in her own pleasure, she set a wild pace, feeling her strength bound high, then higher, as her need swelled.

A free fall through space, a springboard through time. He'd experienced both, but they were nothing compared with this. Blindly he reached for her, and his hands slid down her slick skin. Just as their palms met, they leaped over the top together.

Perfection. Lazily content, Libby cuddled closer, resting her cheek just over Cal's heart, all but purring as he stroked her hair.

Soothed. Every part of her was content. Body, mind, heart. She wondered how long it was possible for two people to lie curled in bed without food or water. Forever. She smiled to herself. She could almost believe it.

"My parents have a cat," she murmured. "A fat yellow cat named Marigold. He doesn't have an ounce of ambition."

"A male cat named Marigold?"

Still smiling, she ran a hand down his arm. "You met my parents."

"Right."

"Anyway, he lies on the windowsill every afternoon. All afternoon. Right this minute I know exactly how he feels." She stretched, only a little, because even that seemed to require too much effort. "I like your bed, Hornblower."

"I've grown fond of it myself."

They were silent for a while, drifting. "That music." It was playing in her head now, sweet, almost unbearably romantic. "I keep thinking I should recognize it."

"Salvadore Simeon."

"Is he a new composer?"

"Depends on your point of view. Late twenty-first century."

"Oh." Her bubble burst. Sometimes forever was a very short time. Holding on one last moment, she turned her head to press her lips to his chest. His heart beat there, strong and steady. "Poetry, classical music and aircycles. An interesting combination."

"Is it?"

"Yes, very. I also know you're hooked on soaps and game shows."

"That's research." He grinned as she pushed herself to a sitting position beside him. "I want to be able to speak intelligently on all popular forms of twentieth-century entertainment." He paused a moment, thinking. "Do you suppose they kept archives? I really want to know if Blake and Eva work things out in spite of

Dorian's conniving. Then there's the problem of who's framing Justin for the murder of the evil and despicable Carlton Slade. I vote for the sweet-faced but hardhearted Vanessa."

"Hooked," she said again, and drew her knees up to her chest to grin at him. "Don't you have soaps?"

"Sure. Never took the time to watch. I always figured they were for homeworkers."

"Homeworkers." She repeated it, liking the precise, genderless phrase. "I haven't asked you all those questions." Libby settled her chin on her knees. "When we get back we should finish writing up everything that's happened to you."

He flicked a finger down her arm. "Everything?"

"Everything that applies. While we're doing that, and putting the capsule together, you can fill me in on the future."

"All right." He climbed out of bed. Maybe it would be best if they stayed busy for the next few hours. He started to reach for his pants, then noticed the Polaroid, which had fallen to the floor. "What's this?"

"A camera. Self-developing. You can have a picture in about ten seconds."

"Is that so?" Amused, he turned it over in his hands. He'd been given one for his tenth birthday that could do precisely the same thing—and it had fitted into the palm of his hand. It had also kept the time, reported the temperature and played his favorite music.

"You've got that superior smirk on your face again, Hornblower."

"Sorry. What do you do? Push this button?"

"That's right— No!" But she was too late. He'd already framed her and shot. "Men have been murdered for less."

"I thought you wanted pictures," he said reasonably as he held the developing image in his hand.

"I'm not dressed."

"Yeah." He smiled. "It's not bad," he decided. "One-dimensional, but it gets the point across. A very sexy point across."

Snatching at the sheet, she scrambled to the foot of the bed and made a grab.

"You want to see?" He held the print tantalizingly out of reach but turned it so that Libby saw herself, her arms hooked around her bare legs, her hair tousled, her eyes heavy. "God, I love it when you blush, Libby."

"I'm not blushing." She told herself she wasn't laughing, either, as she tugged on her clothes. Cal set the camera aside and tugged them off her again.

When they left the ship, the shadows were long. After a brief discussion they decided to strap Cal's cycle to the back of the Land Rover and drive back together.

"It's a good idea," Libby allowed. "If we had some rope."

"What for?" Turning a knob under the seat of the cycle, Cal pulled out two thick, hooked straps.

Libby shrugged. "Well, I suppose if you want to do it the easy way." She bent over the back wheel, planted her feet and braced herself.

"What are you doing?"

"I'm going to help you lift it." She took a firm grip and blew the hair out of her eyes. "Well, come on."

Cal tucked his tongue into his cheek. "Okay, but don't strain yourself."

"Do you have any idea how much equipment we lug around on digs?"

He smiled at her. "No."

"Plenty. On three. One, two, three!" She let out an astonished breath as they lifted the cycle shoulder-high. It couldn't have weighed more than thirty pounds. "You're a riot, Hornblower."

"Thanks." He secured the cycle quickly. "You going to let me drive this time?" When she dug the keys out of her pocket and jiggled them, he went into his pitch. "Come on, Libby, there's no one around."

"Be that as it may, you never showed me a driver's license."

"If we're talking technicalities, I don't think it would apply. Libby, if I can pilot that—" he jerked his thumb in the direction of the ship "—I sure as hell can drive this. I want to see what it's like."

She tossed him the keys. "Just remember, this vehicle stays on the ground."

"Got it." As pleased as a kid with a new toy, he settled behind the wheel. "It works with gears, right?"

"I believe so."

"Fascinating. This pedal here?"

"The clutch," she said, and wondered if she'd just taken her life in her hands.

"The clutch, right. That's what disengages the system so that you can change gears. Higher gears for higher speeds. That's the idea, isn't it?"

"The other pedal? The one beside it? That's the brake. Pay attention to the brake, Hornblower. Pay very close attention."

"Don't worry about a thing." He sent her a cocky grin, then turned the key. "See?" They went in reverse for two fast feet before they came to a jarring stop. "Just a minute. I think I've got it now."

"You've got to put it in off-road."

"Off what?"

Though her palms were slightly damp, she showed him. "Take it easy, will you? And try to go forward."

"No problem." The Land Rover bucked the first few feet, causing Libby to grip the dash with both hands and pray. Cal was having the time of his life, and he was a little disappointed when the ride smoothed out. "Nothing to it." He sent her a cocky grin.

"Just watch where you're going. Oh, God!" She tossed her hands in front of her face so that she wouldn't see the tree they were about to ram.

"Are you always a nervous passenger?" he asked conversationally as he maneuvered around the tree.

"I could grow to hate you. I'm sure of it."

"Loosen up, babe. Let's take a little detour."

"Cal, we should—"

"Run for the gusto," he finished. "Isn't that the phrase?"

"I think it's 'Go for the gusto,' but this isn't a beer commercial." She bit her lip and clung to her safety belt. "Anyway, you can keep it. I think I'd rather live a long, dull life."

He plunged down a rocky slope, driving as if he'd been born behind the wheel. "This is the next best thing to flying." He shot her a look. "Well, maybe not the next best, but it's close."

"I think several of my vital organs have jarred loose. Cal, you're going to go right through that—" The water swooshed up, two glittering curtains on either side of the Land Rover. Libby was drenched when he shot up the opposite bank. "Stream," she muttered, dragging her soaked hair out of her eyes.

As wet as she was, he gave a delighted whoop and

swung around to go through the stream again. She heard her own laughter as the water slapped over her a second time.

"You're crazy." They left the ground briefly, then jolted down with a thud. "But you're not dull."

"You know, with a few modifications, this would go over big at home. I can't figure out why they don't make them anymore. If I came up with a prototype I could send my credit rating through the ozone."

"You're not taking it with you. I still have fourteen payments to make."

"Just a thought." He could have driven for hours. But the air was chill and she was beginning to shiver. Cal circled back.

"Do you know where we are?"

"Sure, about twenty degrees northeast of the ship." He tugged on her wet hair. "I told you I could navigate. Tell you what, when we get back we'll take a hot shower. Then we can build a fire and have some of that brandy. Then we can—" He swore and hit the brakes hard. A group of four in hiking gear was a few feet ahead.

"Damn," Libby muttered. "We hardly ever get anyone this close in so early in the season." It took only a glance for her to determine that the price tags had hardly been removed from the packs and boots.

"If they hike much farther in that direction, they'll be on top of the ship."

Libby swallowed a bubble of panic and smiled as the group approached. "Hello."

"Well, hi there." The man, big, solid and fortyish, leaned on the Land Rover. "You're the first people we've seen since morning."

"We don't get many hikers up this way."

"That's why we picked it. Right, Susie?" He patted a pretty, exhausted-looking woman on the shoulder. Her only answer was a very weary nod. "Rankin. Jim Rankin." He took Cal's hand and pumped it. "My wife, Susie, and our boys, Scott and Joe."

"Nice meeting you. Cal Hornblower. Libby Stone."

"Out four-wheeling it, huh?"

Noting Cal's blank look, Libby said, "Yes, we were about to head in."

"Backpacking's for us." Jim grinned broadly.

It took less than ten seconds to see that only Jim was enthusiastic about tackling the mountains on foot. That might be an advantage. "How far have you come?"

"Started off from Big Vista. Nice little campground, but too crowded. I wanted to show the wife and boys nature in the rough."

Libby judged the boys to be about thirteen and fifteen, and both looked as if they were on the edge of whining. Calculating the distance to the Big Vista campground, she could hardly blame them. "That's quite a hike."

"We're tough. Right, boys?" Both sent him miserable looks.

"You weren't planning to go up this path?" Libby asked, gesturing.

"Matter of fact, we were. Thought we'd try for the ridge before nightfall."

Susie groaned and bent over to massage an aching calf muscle.

"You won't be able to reach it this way. Up ahead's a logging and reforesting area. Did you see the break in the trees?"

"Yeah, I did." He fiddled with the pedometer at his waist. "Wondered about it."

"Harvesting," she said without a blink. "Hiking and camping are off-limits. There's a five-hundred-dollar fine," she added for good measure.

"Well, I sure do appreciate you letting us know."

"Dad, can't we go to a hotel?" one of the boys asked.

"One with a pool," the other chimed in. "And a video arcade."

"And a bed," his wife murmured. "A real bed."

Jim offered Cal and Libby a wink. "Family gets a little cranky this time of day. Wait till you see that sun come up tomorrow, gang. It'll all be worth it."

"There's an easy trail to the west." Libby rose out of

her seat to rest her hip on the side of the Land Rover. "Do you see it?"

"Yeah." Jim didn't like adjusting his itinerary, but the five hundred had done the trick.

She was glad she could give them one with a gradual incline. "Another, oh, three-four miles, and there's a clearing, makes a good campsite. The view's fabulous. You shouldn't have any trouble making it before sundown."

"We could give you a lift." Cal had noted the tired, sulky look on the younger boy's face. The moment the offer was out, it lifted into an engaging grin.

"Oh, no, no, thanks all the same." Jim beamed. "That would be cheating, wouldn't it?"

"Maybe." Susie shifted her pack on her aching back. "But it might just save your life." She nudged her husband aside and leaned toward Cal. "Mr. Hornblower, if you drive us to that campsite, you can name your price."

"Now, Susie—"

"Shut up, Jim." She grabbed a hunk of Cal's damp shirt. "Please. I've got four hundred and fifty-eight dollars' worth of gear on my back. It's yours."

With a hearty laugh, Jim put a hand on his wife's arm. "Now, Susie. We agreed—"

"All bets are off." Her voice rose shrilly. In an obvious effort to control it, she drew a deep breath. "I'm dying here, Jim. I think the boys might be traumatized for life. You don't want to be responsible for that, do you?" Because she wasn't entirely sure of his answer, she jerked away to tuck each boy under her arms. "You hike it," she said. "But I've got blisters, and I don't think I'll ever regain the feeling in my left leg."

"Suze, if I'd known you felt this way—"

"Fine." She wasn't willing to give him time to finish a single sentence. "Now you do. Come on, guys."

They crammed into the back of the Land Rover. After a moment, Jim settled sadly in with them, his youngest on his lap.

"It's, ah, beautiful country," Libby began as she directed Cal along the trail. "You'll probably appreciate it more after you've rested and eaten." And a great deal more than that, she was sure, when Susie discovered they had circled a couple of miles closer to Big Vista.

"It's certainly full of trees." Susie sighed at the luxury of moving without effort. Because she knew Jim was sulking, she patted his knee. "Are you from around here?"

"Originally." Confident that Cal would find the way now, she shifted to face their passengers. "Cal's from Philadelphia."

"Really?" Susie debated flexing her foot, then decided not to risk it. "So are we. Is this your first time out here, Mr. Hornblower?"

"Yes, I guess you could say it's my first time here."

"Ours, too. We wanted to show our sons a part of the country that was still unspoiled. And we have." She gave her husband's knee another squeeze.

Resilient, Jim swung an arm over the back of the seat. "This is one trip they won't forget."

The boys exchanged looks and rolled their eyes but wisely kept silent. There was still a chance for that hotel.

"So, you're from Philadelphia. What do you think of the Phillies' chances this year?"

Cautious, Cal tried to be noncommittal. "I'm always hopeful."

"That's the ticket." Jim slapped Cal on the shoulder. "If they tighten up the infield and beef up the pitching staff they might have a shot."

Baseball, Cal realized with a grin. At least that was something he could relate to. "It's hard to say about this season, but I figure we'll take our share of pennants in the next couple hundred years."

Jim gave a bark of laughter. "That's taking the long view."

When they reached the clearing, their passengers were all in a more cheerful state of mind. The boys leaped out to chase after a rabbit. Susie stepped out more slowly, still favoring her legs.

"It is beautiful." She looked out over the layers of mountains, where the sun was hanging low. "I can't thank you enough, both of you." She glanced over to where her husband was already yelling at the boys to get busy and gather some firewood. "You saved my husband's life."

"He looked in pretty good shape, actually," Cal commented.

"No. I was going to kill him in his sleep." She smiled as she eased the pack from her back. "Now I won't have to, at least for a couple of days."

Jovial, Jim walked back to give his wife a hug. She winced as he squeezed tender muscles. "I tell you, Suze, a man can really breathe up here."

"For the time being," Susie murmured.

"Not like Philadelphia, bless it. Why don't you two stay for supper? Nothing like eating under the sky."

"You're very welcome to," Susie added. "On tonight's menu are the ever-popular beans, with the addition of hot dogs if the cold pack worked, and for dessert some delicious dehydrated apricots."

"Sounds great." And part of him was tempted to stay, just to sit and listen. He thought the Rankin family as entertaining as any daytime drama. "But we've got to get back."

Libby offered her hand to Susie and added a sympathetic pat. "If you follow the trail to the right it'll take you back to Big Vista. It's a long hike, but a pretty one."

And one that would take them in the opposite direction from the ship.

"Can't thank you enough." Jim dug into his backpack and pulled out a business card. The gesture had Libby smothering a chuckle. You could take a boy out of the smog, but… "Give me a ring when you get back, Hornblower. I'm sales manager at Bison Motors. Cut you and the little woman a good deal, new or used."

"I'll keep it in mind." They climbed back into the Land Rover, offered a wave, then left the Rankins behind. "New or used what?" Cal asked Libby.

Chapter 12

Cal thought quite a bit about the Rankins. He had asked Libby if they were an average American family. Her response had been amused. If there was such a phenomenon, she'd told him, they probably fit it.

They interested him perhaps because he saw several parallels between them and his own family. His father, though no one would ever have confused him with big, beaming Jim Rankin, had always had a love of nature, unspoiled land and family trips. Like the other boys, Cal and Jacob had spent a good deal of time sulking, whining and rolling their eyes. And when the chips were down and the limit was reached, it had always been Cal's mother who had laid down the law.

Families, it seemed, were consistent over time. It was a comforting thought.

They had had their fire and brandy when they had returned to the cabin. Then, because Libby was always one to organize, they had gone up to her machine to finish the report.

They would need three copies. The first for the capsule, the second for the ship—and Cal—and the third for Libby.

He'd had to admire her style when he'd read over what she'd done. There was no doubt in his mind that the scientists of his time would find Libby's report both concise and fascinating. The rest was largely technical, and though he knew she couldn't understand the calculations he was feeding her, she typed them out.

They'd spent hours over it, refining, perfecting, taking long periods when she would question him on the social, the political, the cultural climate of his time. She made him think about things he had taken for granted, about others he had casually ignored.

Yes, there was still poverty, but shelters and programs provided the very poor with a roof and a meal. There was still conflict, but all-out war had been avoided for more than 120 years. Politics were still argued over, babies were still cuddled. People complained that the skyways were too crowded. As far as Cal remembered there had been four, or it might have been five, women who had held the office of president.

The more questions he answered, the more she thought of. They fell asleep tangled together in bed in the middle of one of his answers.

They finished the time capsule late the next morning, filling the airtight steel box Libby had bought in town with what seemed most pertinent. One copy of the report was wrapped in plastic before they set it inside. Libby added one of her mother's woven mats and a clay bowl her father had made when she'd been a baby. They added a newspaper, a popular weekly magazine and, at Cal's insistence, a wooden spoon from the kitchen drawer. She added one of the two pictures she'd taken of his ship.

"We need more," Libby muttered.

"I wanted this." He held up a tube of toothpaste. "And I was hoping for some of your underwear."

"Yes to the first, no to the second."

"It's for science," he reminded her.

"Not a chance. We need a tool. We're always very pleased when we find a tool on a dig." She rummaged through a drawer and came up with a screwdriver, a small ball peen hammer and a pipe wrench. "Take your pick."

He took the wrench. "How about a book?"

"Terrific." She dashed into the living room and began

combing the shelves. "I want popular fiction, something written in this era. Ah...Stephen King."

"I've read him. Terrifying."

"Horror transcends time, as well." She brought it into the kitchen and placed it in the box. "If they do any tests, they'll be able to date all of this material. It will back up your story. Come on outside, we'll take some pictures."

Because he got to the camera before her, Cal claimed his right to take the first shots. He snapped the cabin, Libby and the cabin, Libby beside the Land Rover, in the Land Rover. Libby laughing at him. And yelling at him.

"Do you know how much film you've used?" Blowing out a breath, she ripped open another pack. "This stuff averages a dollar a shot. Anthropology's a fascinating field, but the pay's lousy."

"Sorry." He moved to the front of the cabin when she waved with the back of her hand. "I never thought to ask. What's your credit rating?"

"I have no idea." She took a shot of him standing, thumbs hooked in the pockets of his borrowed jeans. "We don't do things that way now. At least I think credit rating means something else. Now it's a matter of what you're worth, or what you make. Annual salary and that sort of thing." She was enough her parents' child that she rarely gave it much thought. "Why don't you unstrap your cycle and sit on it in front of the cabin? A now-and-then sort of thing."

He obliged. "Libby, I don't have any way to pay you back, in your currency, for all of this."

"Don't be silly. It was only a joke."

"There's a great deal more I can't pay you back for."

"There's nothing to pay back." She lowered the camera and weighed each word carefully. "Don't think of it as an obligation. Please. And don't look at me like that. I'm not ready to be serious."

"We don't have much time left."

"I know." She hadn't understood everything he'd dictated to her the night before, but she knew he would be gone before the sun rose the next day. "Let's not spoil what we have." She looked away to give herself a moment to regain her balance. "It's a shame this model doesn't have a timer. It would be nice to get a couple of pictures with both of us in them."

"Hold on." He walked around the side of the building, returning a few moments later with a garden hoe. "Sit on the steps," he told her, then proceeded to strap the camera to the seat of his cycle. He leaned over, checking and adjusting until he had Libby in frame. "Got it." Pleased with himself, he jogged over to sit beside her. He wrapped an arm around her shoulders. "Smile."

She already was.

He used the staff of the hoe to press the button, grinning when he heard the shutter click. The print slid out.

"Very inventive, Hornblower."

"Don't move."

He retrieved the first print, settled back beside her and pressed again.

"One for you, one for the box." He set both prints aside. "And one for me." He tipped her face up to his with his finger and kissed her.

"You forgot to take the picture," she murmured many moments later.

"Oh, yeah." His lips curved against hers as he poked with the hoe.

She took the first print in her hand and studied it. They looked happy, she thought. Happy, ordinary people. It meant a great deal to her now, and would mean even more to her later. She continued to hold it as she rose. "We'd better go bury the capsule."

They strapped it on the back of the cycle so that Libby was sandwiched between it and Cal's back. When they reached the stream, he slipped off and frowned at the shovel she handed him.

"This tool is very primitive. Are you sure there's no easier way?"

"Not in this century, Hornblower." She pointed down. "Dig."

"You can have the first turn."

"That's all right." She sat on the ground and tucked up her legs. "I wouldn't want to deprive you."

She watched him put his back into it. What would he use, she wondered, to dig it up again? How would he feel when he opened it? He would be thinking of her, she knew that. And he would miss her. She hoped he would sit in this same spot and read the letter she had tucked into the box. She'd made certain he hadn't seen her put it in.

It was only a page, but she'd put her heart on it.

She cupped her chin in her hand, listened to the water's music and remembered every word.

Cal. When you read this, you'll be home. I want you to know how happy I am for you. I can't claim to understand what it was like for you to find yourself here, away from everything familiar, separated from your family and friends. But I wanted you to know that in my heart I wanted you to be where you belonged.

I don't know if I can make you understand what the time I've had with you has meant to me. I love you so much, Caleb. It overwhelms me. There won't be a day that goes by that I won't think of you. But I won't be unhappy. Please don't think of me, or remember me that way. What you gave to me in these few days is more than I ever imagined, all I ever needed. Whenever I look at the sky, I'll picture you.

I'll still study the past to try to understand why man is what he is. Now, having known you, I'll always have hope for what he can become.

Be happy. I want to know you are. Don't forget me. I wanted to put a sprig of rosemary in the capsule, but I was afraid it would only turn to dust. Find some, and think of me. "Pray, love, remember."

Libby

"Libby?" Cal leaned against the shovel, watching her.

"Yes?"

"Where were you?"

"Oh, not very far away." Glancing down, she lifted a brow. "Well, I knew a big strong man like you could dig a hole."

"I think I have a blister."

"Aw." She rose to kiss the tender skin between his thumb and forefinger. "Let's put it in. Then you can watch while I cover it up."

"Good idea." The moment the box was in, he handed her the shovel. Libby eyed it, then the pile of dirt that had to be replaced.

"Four women presidents?"

He stretched his tired back. "Might have been five."

With a nod, Libby began to shovel. "Cal?"

"Hmm?" He was giving serious consideration to a nice, lazy nap.

"The questions I asked before, those were the big ones, the sweeping ones. I wondered if I could ask you something more personal."

"Probably."

"Would you tell me about your family?"

"What would you like to know?"

"Who they are, what they're like." She tossed dirt into the hole in a steady rhythm that Cal enjoyed. "I'd like to imagine I knew them a little."

"My father's a research and development technician. Lab work, all indoors and confining. He's very dedicated, dependable. At home he likes to garden, plants flowers from seed and works them all by hand."

As he drew in the scent of the freshly turned earth that Libby worked, Cal could almost see his father cultivating his garden.

"Sometimes he paints. Really, *really* bad landscapes and still lifes. He even knows they're bad, but he claims art doesn't have to be good to be art. He's always threatening to hang one of them in the house. He's...I don't know, steady. I doubt I've heard him raise his voice more than a dozen times in my life. But you listen to him. He's like the adhesive that kept the family centered."

He stretched out on the grass to watch the sky as he

continued. "My mother is…what was that term you used once? Wired? She's packed with energy and a blazing intellect that's almost scary. She intimidates a lot of people. She's always amused by that. I guess because inside she's soft as butter. She raised her voice plenty, but she always felt guilty about it. Jacob and I gave her a hell of a time.

"In her free time she likes to read—flashy novels or impossibly technical books. She's chief counsel for the United Ministry of Nations, so she's always poring over some six-inch pile of legal documents."

"The United Ministry of Nations?"

"I guess you'd call it an extension of the UN. It had to be expanded in…hell, I don't know when. I think it was expanded because of the colonies and settlements."

"It sounds like a very prestigious position." Libby discovered she was already intimidated.

"Yes. She thrives on it. On the work and the worry. She's got a great laugh—one of those big fill-the-room kind of laughs. They met in Dublin. She was practicing law there, and my father went over for a vacation. They matched and ended up in Philadelphia."

Libby tamped down the dirt. It had been impossible not to hear the affection in his voice, impossible not to understand it. "What about your brother?"

"Jacob. He's…intense is a good word. He gets his brain from my mother, and his temperament, she claims, from her grandfather. You're never quite sure with J.T. whether he's going to grin at you or throw a punch. He studied law and then, when he'd had his fill of it, dived into astrophysics. He collects problems so that he can pick them apart. He's a sonofabitch," Cal said affectionately, "but he has my father's unswerving, immeasurable sense of loyalty."

"Do you like them?" When Cal looked up, she elaborated. "What I mean is, most people love their family, but they aren't necessarily friends with them. I wondered if you liked them."

"Yes, I do." He watched as she strapped the shovel back on the cycle. "They'd like you."

"I could meet them if you took me with you." She bit her lip the moment the words were out. She couldn't turn around to look at him. She couldn't have said just when the thought had hatched in her mind.

"Libby—" He was up and standing behind her, his hands hovering over her shoulders.

"I've studied the past," she said quickly, turning and gripping his forearms. "If you let me come with you, it would give me the chance to study the future."

He framed her face with his hands. There was a glint of tears in her eyes. "And your family?"

"They'd understand. I'd leave them a letter, try to explain."

"They'd never believe you," he said quietly. "They'd

spend years looking for you, wondering if you were still alive. Libby, can't you see that's what's tearing me apart about my own? They don't know where I am or what's happened to me. I know by now they're waiting to hear if I'm dead or alive."

"I'll make them understand." She heard the desperation in her own voice and fought to steady it. "If they know I'm happy, that I'm doing what I want to do, they'll be satisfied with that."

"Maybe. Yes, if they were sure. But I can't take you, Libby."

She made her hands drop away and stepped back. "No, of course not. I don't know what I was thinking of. I got caught up—"

"Damn it, don't." Grabbing her arms, he hauled her against him. "Don't think I don't want you, because I do. It's not a choice of right or wrong, Libby. If I could be sure, if there were no risks involved, I might toss you on the damn ship whether you wanted to go with me or not."

"Risks?" She'd stiffened at the word, and now she drew back. "What risks?"

"Nothing's foolproof."

"Don't treat me like a fool. What risks?"

He let out a long breath. There was a calculation he hadn't given her the night before. "The probability factor for a successful time warp is 76.4."

"76.4," she repeated. "It doesn't take a genius to figure out that leaves 23.6 as the factor for failure. What happens if you fail?"

"I don't know." But he could make a good guess. Frying in the sun's gravitational pull was one of the less painful possibilities. "And I won't take chances with you, no matter how much I want you with me."

She wasn't going to panic, because panic wouldn't help. Taking three deep breaths, she felt some balance return. "Caleb, if you gave yourself a little more time, do you think you could narrow the odds?"

"Maybe. Probably," he conceded. "Libby, I'm running out of time. The ship's already been in the open for two weeks. It was blind luck that we headed off the Rankins yesterday. What do you think would happen to me, to us, if it were found? If I were found?"

"The real season doesn't start for weeks. We hardly get more than a dozen hikers in a year."

"It only takes one."

He was right, and she knew it. They'd been living on borrowed time right from the start. "I'll never know, will I?" She traced a finger under the fading wound on his brow. "Whether you made it."

"I'm a good pilot. Trust me." He kissed her fingers. "And it'll be easier for me to concentrate if I'm not worried about you."

"It's hard to argue with common sense." She worked

up a smile. "I know you said you had a few last details to see to at the ship. I'm just going to walk back to the cabin."

"I won't be long."

"Take your time." She needed some of her own. "I'll fix a bon voyage supper." She started off at an easy gait, then called over her shoulder, "Oh, Hornblower, pick me some flowers."

He picked an armful. It wasn't easy balancing them as he flew the cycle. The path beneath him was strewn with white and pink and pale blue blossoms. He thought they smelled like her—fresh, earthy, exotic.

In the hours he'd worked aboard ship one thought had run continually through his mind. She'd been willing to go with him. To leave her home. Not just her home, he corrected. Her life.

Perhaps it had been impulse, something that had been born of the moment.

Reasons didn't matter. He needed to hold on to that one sweet thought. She'd been willing to go with him.

He saw only the faintest light through the kitchen window. That had him frowning as he stored his bike and retrieved a few of the fallen flowers. Perhaps she'd decided to take a nap or was waiting for him in the front of the cabin by the fire.

He liked the idea of seeing her there, curled up on the

couch under one of her mother's exquisite throws. She'd be reading, her eyes a little sleepy behind her glasses.

Pleased with the image, he opened the door and found a completely different, and even more alluring, one.

She was waiting for him. But it was candlelight. She was still lighting them, dozens of them, all pure white. The table was set for two, and a bottle of champagne sat nestled in a clear bucket. The room smelled of candles, of the spices she'd used for cooking, and of her.

She turned to smile at him, and he felt the breath quite simply leave his body.

Her hair was swept up off her neck so that he could see the long, delicate curve. She wore a dress the color of moonlight that glittered at the bodice as she moved. It left her shoulders bare, then slipped like a lover down her hips and thighs.

"You remembered." She crossed to him, holding out her arms for the flowers. He didn't move a muscle. "Are they for me?"

"What? Yes." Like a man in a trance, he offered them to her. "There were more when I started out."

"This is more than enough." She had a vase waiting, and she filled it. "Dinner's almost ready. I hope you like it."

"You dazzle me, Liberty."

She turned back, electrified by what she saw in his

eyes. "I wanted to, just once." When he just continued to stare, her shyness rose up and had her twisting her fingers. "I bought the champagne and the dress while I was in town yesterday. I thought it would be nice to do something a little special tonight."

"I'm afraid if I move you'll vanish."

"No." She offered her hand and gripped hard when he took it. "I'll stay right here. Why don't you open the bottle?"

"I want to kiss you first."

Her heart went into her smile as she wound her arms around his neck. "All right. Just once."

They ate. But the trouble she had gone to over the meal was wasted. They didn't know what they were tasting. Champagne was superfluous. They were already drunk on each other. The candles burned down low while they lingered.

They carried some up to the bedroom, filling the room with the soft, flickering light so that they could watch each other as they loved.

There was sweetness, slow, savoring sweetness. There was urgency, fevered, racing urgency. There was power and tenderness, demand and generosity.

Hour melted into hour, but they never drew apart. Each tremble, each sigh, each heartbeat would be remembered. The candles guttered out, but they were still wrapped together.

Then, though the words were never spoken, they knew it was the last time. His hands seemed that much more gentle, her lips that much softer.

When it was over, the beauty left her weak and weepy. In defense, she curled against him and prayed for sleep. She couldn't bear to watch him go.

He lay still, wakeful until the first faint hints of light crept into the room. He was grateful she slept; he would never have been able to say goodbye. When he rose it hurt, a sharp, sweet ache that rocked him. Moving quickly, struggling to keep his mind blank, he pulled on the jumpsuit she'd set out for him.

Afraid of waking her, he touched only her hair, then moved quietly out of the room. Libby opened her eyes only when she heard the soft click of the cabin door. Turning her face into the pillow, she let the tears come.

The ship was secured, and the calculations were plotted. Cal sat on the bridge and watched night fade. It was important that he take off before sunrise. He had the timing down to a millisecond. There was little room for error. His life depended on it.

But his thoughts kept drifting back to Libby. Why hadn't he known it would hurt this badly to leave? Yet he had to leave. His life, his time, weren't here with hers. There was no use going over again what he had already agonized over a dozen times.

Still, he sat while precious moments clicked away.

Prepare for standard orbital flight.

"Yes," he told the computer absently. Instruments began to hum. In a way that was second nature to him, Cal prepared for takeoff. He paused again, staring at the viewscreen.

All systems ready. Ignition at your discretion.

"Right. Commence countdown."

Commencing. Ten, nine, eight, seven...

From the kitchen doorway, Libby heard the rumble. Impatient, she rubbed tears from her eyes and strained to see. There was a flash. She thought she caught a quick glint of metal streaking across the lightening sky. Then it was gone. The woods were quiet again.

She shivered. She wished she could convince herself it was because the air was chill and she was wearing only her short blue robe.

"Be safe," she murmured. Then gave in and allowed herself the luxury of a few more tears.

Life went on, she lectured herself. The birds were beginning to sing. The sun was nearly up.

She wanted to die.

That was nonsense. Shaking herself, she set the kettle on to boil. She was going to have a cup of tea, wash the dishes they'd been too careless to notice the night before. Then she was going back to work.

She would work until she couldn't keep her eyes open, and then she would sleep. She would get up again and work again until her dissertation was complete. It would be the best damn paper her colleagues had ever read. And then she'd travel.

And she would miss him until the day she died.

When the kettle boiled, she poured her tea, then sat with it at the kitchen table. After a moment, she shoved it aside, laid her head on her folded hands and wept again.

"Libby."

She knocked the chair over as she rose. He was there, standing in the doorway, fatigue all over his face and something, something much more powerful, in his eyes. She rubbed hers. He couldn't be there.

"Caleb?"

"Why are you crying?"

She heard him. Dazed, she pressed a hand against her ear. "Caleb." She repeated. "But how—I heard, I saw— You're gone."

"Have you been crying since I left?" He stepped toward her but only touched a fingertip to her damp cheek.

His touch was real. If she was mad, she accepted it. "I don't understand. How can you be here?"

"I have a question to ask you first." He dropped his

hands to his sides. "Just one question. Are you in love with me?"

"I—I need to sit down."

"No." He caught her arm and held her still. "I want an answer. Are you in love with me?"

"Yes. Only an idiot would have to ask."

He smiled, but his grip held firm. "Why didn't you ever tell me?"

"Because I didn't want—I knew you had to go." Dizzy, she put a hand to her head. "Let me sit."

He released her, then watched her sink unsteadily into a chair.

"I haven't slept," she murmured, as if to herself. "I suppose I could be hallucinating."

He tilted her head back, then planted a hard, bruising kiss on her mouth. Before he could stop himself, he dragged her halfway out of the chair. "Is that real enough for you?"

"Yes," she said weakly. "Yes. But I don't understand. How can you be here?"

He let her go again. "I rode the cycle."

"No, I mean…" What did she mean? "I was standing at the door. I heard you take off. I even saw, just a glimpse, but I saw the ship in the sky."

"I sent it back. The computer's at the helm."

"You sent it back," she repeated slowly. "Oh, my God, Caleb, why?"

"Only an idiot would have to ask."

Her eyes filled and spilled over. "No, not for me. I can't bear it. Your family—"

"I left a disk for them. I told them everything, a great deal more than what's in the report I left on board. Where I was, why I had to stay. If the ship makes it back, and it has as good a chance without me as it did with me, they'll understand."

"I can't ask you to do this."

"You didn't." He took her hand before she could turn away again. "You would have gone with me, wouldn't you, Libby?"

"Yes."

"I might have taken you up on that if I'd been sure we would have lived through it. Listen to me." He drew her to her feet. "I'd started countdown. I'd convinced myself that my life was back there where I'd left it. There were a dozen logical reasons why I had to go. And there was one, only one, reason I had to stay. I love you. My life is here." He tightened his grip, brought her close. "I came through time for you, Libby. Don't ever, ever think I made a mistake."

She shook her head. "I'm afraid you'll think so."

"'Time is... Time was... Time is past,'" he murmured. "My time is in the past, Libby. With you."

Her eyes filmed over again. "I love you so much, Caleb. I'll make you happy."

"I'm counting on it." He picked her up, pausing to capture her mouth in a long, long kiss. "You need sleep," he told her. "Real sleep."

"No, I don't."

He laughed, and the last vestige of tension fled. He was exactly where he belonged. "We'll see. Later we'll talk about how we're going to handle the rest of this."

"Rest?"

"The marriage-and-family part I can handle."

"You haven't asked me yet."

"I'll get around to it. Anyway, I'm going to need new ID. Then I've got to get a job. Something with a—an annual salary, right?"

"Something you enjoy," she corrected. "That's more important than salary and group hospitalization."

"Group what?"

"Don't worry about it." She nuzzled into his neck. "I suppose Dad could give you some kind of position until you figure it all out."

"I don't think I want to make tea." Suddenly inspired, he stopped by the side of the bed. "Tell me, how do you go about getting a pilot's license around here?"

* * * * *

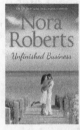
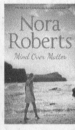
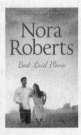
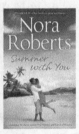
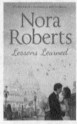
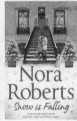
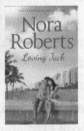

MILLS & BOON®

Why shop at millsandboon.co.uk?

Each year, thousands of romance readers find their perfect read at millsandboon.co.uk. That's because we're passionate about bringing you the very best romantic fiction. Here are some of the advantages of shopping at www.millsandboon.co.uk:

* **Get new books first**—you'll be able to buy your favourite books one month before they hit the shops

* **Get exclusive discounts**—you'll also be able to buy our specially created monthly collections, with up to 50% off the RRP

* **Find your favourite authors**—latest news, interviews and new releases for all your favourite authors and series on our website, plus ideas for what to try next

* **Join in**—once you've bought your favourite books, don't forget to register with us to rate, review and join in the discussions

Visit **www.millsandboon.co.uk**
for all this and more today!

MILLS_WEB